Layla in the Sky with Diamonds

Layla in the Sky with Diamonds

Manbeena Bhullar Sandhu

Copyright © 2017 Manbeena Bhullar Sandhu.

All rights reserved. No part of this book may be used or reproduced by any means, graphic, electronic, or mechanical, including photocopying, recording, taping or by any information storage retrieval system without the written permission of the author except in the case of brief quotations embodied in critical articles and reviews.

This is a work of fiction. All of the characters, names, incidents, organizations, and dialogue in this novel are either the products of the author's imagination or are used fictitiously.

Archway Publishing books may be ordered through booksellers or by contacting:

Archway Publishing
1663 Liberty Drive
Bloomington, IN 47403
www.archwaypublishing.com
1 (888) 242-5904

Because of the dynamic nature of the Internet, any web addresses or links contained in this book may have changed since publication and may no longer be valid. The views expressed in this work are solely those of the author and do not necessarily reflect the views of the publisher, and the publisher hereby disclaims any responsibility for them.

Any people depicted in stock imagery provided by Thinkstock are models, and such images are being used for illustrative purposes only. Certain stock imagery © Thinkstock.

ISBN: 978-1-4808-4191-8 (sc)
ISBN: 978-1-4808-4192-5 (hc)
ISBN: 978-1-4808-4190-1 (e)

Library of Congress Control Number: 2017900501

Print information available on the last page.

Archway Publishing rev. date: 1/31/2017

Contents

1. Living Is Easy With Eyes Closed — 1
2. People Are Strange — 13
3. Strange Days — 23
4. This Is the End — 37
5. San Francisco — 45
6. Light My Fire — 52
7. India, India — 67
8. Hello! I Love You — 78
9. Till the Heavens Stop the Rain — 89
10. I'm Only Sleeping — 97
11. Oh, My Love — 106
12. I'm Going Away — 124
13. Our Love Becomes a Funeral Pyre — 140

14. There's a Killer on the Road	150
15. Into This World We're Thrown	160
16. End of the Night	169
17. The End	177

Chapter 1

Living Is Easy With Eyes Closed

Living is easy with eyes closed,
misunderstanding all you see,
It's getting hard to be someone, but it all works out,
It doesn't matter much to me.

— *John Lennon*

1985 India

John Lennon hummed "Strawberry Fields" in Layla's ears through her puffy headphones as she lay in a semi-comatose state on the Air India seat. They were travelling Poona to Delhi. Her partly open and welled-up blue eyes glittered like glass, and her slightly open lips were dry and chapped. Her wavy blonde hair fell carelessly over her face and shoulders. Jovan lay still on the seat beside her, pressing his warm cheek against the bare, cold skin of his mommy's trembling arm. Then he turned his head and stared deep into Jim Morrison's eyes tattooed on Mommy's left arm. The god of rock stared back. Jove and Jimmy had played this game many a time. Those nights when Layla was passed out and unable to listen to her son, the star in the tattoo on her arm stayed awake and listened. He played God to Jovan. God, who did not even blink. His wild hair had wiped Jovan's tears numerous times when Jovan had chosen Mommy's left shoulder to cry on.

Curled up on the airplane seat, Layla watched Jovan and Jenna through her half-closed eyes as she lay in agony, sweating and freezing. She was sweating to the point of dehydration, interspersed with shivering and goosebumps. Music was not helping either. Breathless and frustrated, she removed her headphones with her shaky hands, crouched over, and pulled out a bag that was tucked under the front seat. She shoved her headphones inside the bag and pulled out a maroon shawl. She hastily wrapped herself up to her ears in it with trembling hands.

A curtain fell over Jim the God's face as Jovan watched motionlessly. He pondered a bit and then thought of playing with Bhagwan, who rested on Layla's bosom atop her shawl, gently riding the up-and-down motion of her breath. Bhagwan looked intensely towards the heavens, framed inside a glittering gold-rimmed locket joined to a necklace of 108 rosewood beads that hung loosely around Layla's nape. Jovan looked carefully at Mommy's mala for a moment before his body stiffened. Anxiety stemming from his recent nightmare grew to fear and then terror. He started grinding his teeth and clenching his fists. "Go away, bad dream. Go away," he bellowed.

"Hey! What's the matter with you, you nincompoop?" yelled Jenna, hitting Jovan on the head with her *Nancy Drew* mystery book, ruffling more of his straggly hair. "I was in middle of a petrifying, blood-curdling, and bone-chilling scene." She grunted, and her big brown eyes pierced Jovan through her horn-rimmed spectacles, demanding an explanation. "What happened?" She glared at him, shaking her bangs and her two slithering pigtails.

"I had a bad dream last night," mumbled Jovan, looking rather sheepishly toward Jenna. "Like … I saw Mommy hanging by her *mala,* which had turned into a noose, under a banyan tree in a dark night. She was *dead.*" Two sets of four eyes stared motionlessly into each other's in brief, eerie silence before Jovan's dewy eyes gave way to a tear that trickled down his stern left cheek.

Jenna's heart melted and then strengthened. She sighed. "You silly Billy, it's just a dream," she reassured Jovan with a warm hug. "Now, in the future, quit asking Lakshmi to narrate ghost stories to you at night, okay?" She lovingly yet forcefully waved her index finger at Jovan.

"Okay," mumbled Jovan meekly.

"Pinkie promise?"

"Pinkie promise."

Layla listened and helplessly watched the duo. Her muscles ached, and her stomach cramped. She was thirsty. She extended her tremulous hand to grab a bottle of Bisleri filtered water. She supported the end of the teetering bottle with her left hand to control the shaking as she gulped a hurried sip that refused to go down. She wanted to throw up! She wanted to die! She needed cocaine! It had been twenty-four hours since Layla had last had coke in her system. Italian Prem was supposed to bring a stash for her to the German bakery before she'd boarded the flight to Delhi. But damn him, he did not show up, leaving Layla feeling angry, betrayed, disheartened, and desperate.

Sickly impatient and shivering in the airplane seat, Layla stared at her watch. The hands didn't seem to move. Twenty more minutes before she would land in Delhi, and forty more before she could see Handsome Leonardo, who would cure her illness. An hour in all to go—but an hour felt like eternity to Layla at this moment.

Jovan grabbed hold of Mommy's hemp bag, rummaged through it, and took out a gilded mirror. He tried fixing his curly locks that Jenna's *Nancy Drew* had wrecked. Jovan was proud of his decorated mass of curls, styled after Jim Morrison. He walked, talked, and sang like the lizard king in a 7-year-old's body. And he meditated like Bhagwan. He knew how to sit in a lotus posture and breathe in and out. Jovan loved his mommy, and in order to gain her attention, he modelled himself after her two heroes, the god of rock Jim Morrison and the controversial spiritual guru Bhagwan, who had disciples swarming to him from all over the globe like bees to honey. Jovan sang and jived on "Break on Through (to the Other Side)" while wearing his tiny concho belt over his tiny leather pants. The fancy clothing set was a treasured gift from his maternal grandparents who lived in New York. Jenna and Meera, the maid Lakshmi's daughter, danced around him wildly like desperate fans desiring a glance and one touch of his finger as Jovan rocked and rolled in a trance, like Jimmy.

Jovan also played "The Meditation Game," posing as Bhagwan holding court in his diamond-studded sparkling Swiss watch and Gucci sunglasses. As a replacement for the Swiss and the Gucci, Jovan had bought his plastic sunglasses and his plastic watch from Vinod, a street vendor who sold cheap plastic toys in all bright colours—orange, pink, yellow, and green. Vinod tooted his bright orange plastic horn each Sunday morning as he cycled through the streets of Koregaon Park, enticing kids with his plastic treasures. The toot of his horn caught the children in their tracks; in the middle of playing hopscotch, hide-and-seek, or marbles, they solidified like statues at the sight of Vinod. When the spell broke, they clamoured around his bicycle. Tiny hands reached out for tiny treasures: one rupee for the horn, two rupees for the boat, four rupees for the doll. Jovan bought the sunglasses for two rupees and the watch for one rupee. Then he held court as Bhagwan every Sunday afternoon under the banyan tree, sitting on a throwaway dental chair. Other children who squatted on the ground at his feet played the role of *sannyasins* (disciples), like his mommy, Layla, aka Ma Prem Leela.

Bhagwan had bestowed this name upon Layla when she took initiation as his disciple eight years ago. "Layla will now become Ma Prem Leela," he had announced blissfully, "meaning 'love with divine play.'" He lovingly placed the mala around Layla's nape and touched her third-eye chakra. Tears of overwhelming joy trickled down Layla's cheeks as other sannyasins, clad in orange robes, joyously sang and danced around her under a shower of flowers. She kneeled with folded palms in front of Bhagwan. "Universe is singing a song, universe is dancing along, universe is singing on a day like this, and it's high time to dance, so wake up and dance …" Ma Prem Leela danced away to glory from that day onwards. Hence, Layla Smith, born of thoroughbred American parents, became Ma Prem Leela that glorious day.

Jovan glared at Mommy's mala again. He wrinkled the corners of his mouth and made a sad, droopy face. "Jenna, do you think Mommy loves Bhagwan more than us?" he asked, looking mournfully towards her.

"Jove, do you think it rains diamonds on Saturn and Jupiter?" asked Jenna.

"Wow! Does it?" questioned Jovan.

"Yes, it does!" answered Jenna.

"But that's not an answer to my question," Jovan protested vehemently.

"Your question is not worth being dignified with an answer," retorted Jenna. Jenna usually brushed away questions and comments that evoked mixed feelings in her. She did not like confronting could-be-true facts.

All of a sudden, Jovan started sobbing, experiencing a strange brew of emotions: boredom, frustration, neglect, anger, and now being yelled at by someone who always stood by him. Jenna's tender heart melted again at seeing Jovan cry. She made a sad, pitying face, leaned towards him, and wrapped him in her caring arms. Though only 2 years older than Jovan, he being 7 and she being 9, Jenna played the responsible big sister for the little guy.

Jovan peered out of the airplane window. According to Mommy, when people died, they lived amongst the stars and the moon, and they walked on the clouds. Jovan looked carefully and believed he saw Rani playing amongst the clouds. Rani was their chauffer, Sohan Singh's daughter. She was a dear friend to Jovan and Jenna before she was mercilessly burned to death a year before, during the riots that followed the assassination of the Indian prime minister. Rani and her mother were visiting relatives in Delhi when the riots broke out, and they were both burned alive that night. Sohan Singh was the only one in the family who had survived because he was in Chandigarh, serving Jenna's grandparents, when the riots broke out. He was a devastated man and now cared for Jenna and Jovan like his own children.

When Jovan had questioned Mommy as to why Rani was killed, Mommy simply stated, "People kill innocent lives in the name of love and religion." Jovan had spent many nights trying to figure out how someone could kill in the name of love and religion. He had found no answer. Standing amidst the clouds, Rani waved Jovan a gentle goodbye with a pixie smile on her lips and a halo around her head. Jovan waved back. Jovan then imagined John Lennon singing as he strode through the clouds "Imagine there are no countries, it isn't hard to do, nothing to kill or die for, and no religion too. Imagine all the people living life in peace ..." Jovan smiled and waved him goodbye as he continued humming. "Living life in peace ..." The song made Jovan feel good and cheered him up.

One fine day, Mommy had also told Jenna and Jovan that she did not agree with the superficial ways of the world. She believed in neither war nor in the idea of being a slave to the clock. She was a misfit in this world and was happy to be one. She did not believe in "the system," so she had chosen to drop out of it. She was a rebel, a flower child of the '60s and '70s who had protested capitalist values then, and now she was a *Sannyasin* of the '80s who chose to live life according to her own set of ideals.

As Mommy spoke that day with a preposterous amount of zeal and fervour, Jovan and Jenna, who stood pinned to the wall, had watched her with a bit of admiration and a bit of fear. The duo had later discussed that they completely agreed upon and were rather ecstatic with the idea of not favouring the war, but they were not very comfortable with the idea of dropping out of the system. They also pondered whether they were already born dropped out; in that case, they had no option, and it saddened and worried them. Eventually, they decided upon staying optimistic and hoped that one day, when they were grown up, they could find a happy medium. They had ended their discussion with a smile, a hug, and a glimmer of hope.

Jove continued singing softly, and Jenna joined in "You may say I'm a dreamer, but I'm not the only one, I hope someday you'll join us and the world will be as one ..." Their singing was interrupted by the announcement made by the air hostess. "Ladies and gentlemen, kindly tie your seat belts. Shortly we will be starting our descent to Palam Airport, Delhi. The outside air temperature is 35 degrees Celsius coupled with heavy showers."

"Mommy, Mommy! Wake up! We are in Delhi. Wake up!" shouted Jovan excitedly, jolting Layla's body back and forth.

"Oh, okay," she moaned, rubbing her bloodshot eyes as she tried to open them with difficulty. Jovan's wide and warm, missing-tooth smile greeted Layla.

"Are you okay, Mommy?" asked Jenna, looking a little concerned.

"Yes, Sweetheart," Layla managed to answer as she staggered out of her seat.

Jovan and Jenna helped Layla push the luggage cart into a corner as the three of them walked out of the airport gates. It was raining cats and dogs. Layla click opened her umbrella that she was quite used to carrying along at all times during the rainy season, especially after having lived through a number of notorious Goan monsoons. Three of them huddled under it. People stared at them as they walked by. Layla was quite used to Indian eyes scanning her from head to toe. A lofty, blue-eyed blonde with long and wavy wild hair and a beaded mala hanging around the neck was certainly not something to be missed. Layla was a head turner with one white and one brown kid. Jenna was the brown one; she looked nothing like Layla and had taken completely after her purebred Indian father, Gary, aka Gurveer Singh Sandhu. She was black-haired, brown-eyed, and olive-skinned. Jovan was a blue-eyed blond, like his American mommy and his Italian daddy, Riccardo Romano.

Jovan clutched his teddy close to his chest, trying to save it from the downpour. He raised himself on his tippy toes, craned his neck, and wrinkled his forehead in an effort to scan the crowd, searching for Sohan Uncle. Rain formed a blur around them. Water cascaded off their umbrella and found its way into their footwear. Jove and Jenna played the shoe squishing game: whose shoe made more of a squeaky squishy sound when pressed? Jenna won. Layla lifted the hem of her maroon maxi to save it from getting soaked as they zigzagged around the puddles and potholes to a more visible spot. Feeling jittery, she took the front strands of her hair and hurriedly tied them in a knot behind her head with her shaky hands. She was sweating, panting, and shivering all at once. Where was Sohan Singh? Layla looked around frantically, and her patience was running out.

Suddenly she felt someone pull the end of her maroon shawl that she had wrapped around her backless back. "Paisa madam, hungry," muttered a little barefoot boy standing exposed in torrential downpour, thrusting his palm towards her.

"Money, please. Baby hungry," wailed a woman in a ripped sari that clung to her as she pressed a child against her breast. Layla hastily poked through her bag, took out a wad of 50-rupee notes, and gave one each to the boy and the woman.

"Thank you, madam, thank you" said the boy gleefully as he ran to inform the rest of his troupe of his triumph.

Soon the three of them were surrounded by little children and women drenched in rain, pulling on to their sleeves, their clothes, and their hair. "Paisa, please. Hungry, no food." "Hungry, madam, paisa." Voices echoed in from all directions, and the noise grated on Layla's nerves. Her head started reeling, and she was going to collapse. Seeing no other way out, she took out a few more bills and managed to yell, "*Chalo hato,* please. No more, all finished. *Chalo,* please." She gestured wildly as she distributed the notes.

A policeman strode towards them, briskly hitting his baton on the concrete floor in a threatening motion. "*Bhago yahan se,*" he shouted. Almost magically, within seconds the group dispersed and disappeared out of sight. A lone woman in a drenched sari flashed Layla a nasty look, muttered something mean, and ambled away.

"Boy, oh boy!" mumbled Layla as the three of them heaved a deep sigh of relief. *Now, where on earth is Sohan Singh?* she wondered.

"Sohan Uncle!" shouted Jovan joyously as he ran towards the tall and well-built turbaned Sikh who was walking towards them under the refuge of his umbrella. Jenna ran behind him. They exchanged friendly fist bumps followed by warm hugs.

"For you baby and *kaka ji,*" said Sohan Sigh as he reached in his shirt pocket and took out two five-star chocolate bars.

"We missed you, Uncle," said Jenna and Jovan joyfully as they chomped on their chocolate bars.

"Me too" replied Sohan as he walked towards Layla. He folded his palms together and bowed his head respectfully. "Sat Sri Akal Madam," he greeted.

"Sat Sri Akal Sohan! All well?" asked Layla.

"Yes, Madam! Sorry I am late—too much traffic. When it rains, there is traffic jam always," he explained in his Punjabi-accented English.

"That's okay, Sohan," said Layla.

Sohan Singh took over the luggage cart from them, walked towards the car, and slid the suitcases in the luggage compartment of the shining black Mercedes. The three passengers flopped in the back seat. "To Taj Palace," instructed Layla.

"Okay, Madam." Sohan Sigh nodded as they drove off.

The costumed bellboy showed them to their suite. Layla ordered a banana split each for the kids through room service as she rushed to room 201, where Handsome Leonardo was staying. She pounded on the door. "Ciao, Bella!" greeted Leonardo, sticking his neck out of the doorway as he kissed Layla on the cheek and ushered her in.

"I need a line, Leonardo. I am dying," said Layla as she flung herself on the comfy armchair in anticipation of the offering.

"*Un momento, prego,*" replied Leonardo as he chopped cocaine on a fancy glass block. His silver streaks of hair were neatly tied in a ponytail. He looked magnificent in his navy-blue velvet pants and velvet vest embroidered in silver. His partly bare chest was well-built and flaunted a tattoo of a roaring lion.

He proffered a mirror with lines of cocaine and offered Layla a rolled-up 100-rupee bill. She extended her eager nose and snorted a line through the rolled-up note. She lolled her head backwards as she melted into the cushioned back of the armchair, and her body relaxed as she reclined. The world felt safer as comfort warmed her blood. She removed her sandals and rubbed the soles of her feet against the velvety softness of the carpet. She could finally think clearly and breathe normally.

"Feeling better, Bella?" asked Handsome Leonardo.

"Yes, thank you, Leo. Much better! Going somewhere?" Layla asked, seeing him dressed to the nines.

"David is throwing a bash at his farmhouse tonight. Come along," he offered.

"Nay! Too tired" she replied, throwing her head sideways.

"Are you going to see Riccardo tomorrow?" he inquired.

"Yes," she replied.

"Okay. He wants you to keep a suitcase safe with you for a couple of days. Monika will come to Chandigarh and will pick it up from you. It has stashes of heroin sealed inside its leather. She is doing a run to Los Angeles," explained Leonardo.

Layla raised her voice and spoke vehemently. "Oh, no! None of this. I'm keeping no suitcase with me. I've got kids, for God's sake."

"I would have kept it with me, Bella, but I'm leaving for Milano tomorrow night, and Monika is not available for pick up till Thursday," said Leonardo, shrugging his shoulders.

"That's not my problem, Leonardo. I'm going to have a word with Riccardo tomorrow," Layla said firmly.

"Okay, see what he says. For now, here is another line for you, Princess," said Leonardo, extending his hand to offer the gilded mirror with fine lines of coke on it.

Layla lowered her face and sniffed the powdered nectar. Leo gave Layla a week's supply for personal use. "Come to me by tomorrow afternoon to pick up the suitcase."

"I'll see," Layla replied as she kissed him goodnight.

Layla stumbled her way unsteadily through the corridor, feeling peachy. She heard giggles as she twisted the door knob of her suite, taking off the "Do Not Disturb" sign. She followed the sound of laughter to the grand bathroom; the sparkling marble floor felt cool beneath her bare feet. Jenna and Jovan were enjoying a lavish bubble bath inside the majestic tub. Jovan played Santa, making a beard of the bubble foam while Jenna sang the Liril Soap jingle. "Laaa, la-la-la laaaa, la-la-la-la laaaa, la-la-la" She wiggled her foamed foot to the tune and snapped her foamed fingers.

Layla joined in the singing as she helped wash, dry, and change the two. They ordered room service, a mozzarella cheese pizza.

Layla relaxed on the arched balcony of her suite and reclined on a cushioned cane sofa with her legs stretched out on the futon in front, smelling the fragrance of the night-blooming jasmine mixed with the scent of the moist earth. The children lay sound asleep on the king-sized bed as she watched them through the curved space between tasselled drapery adorning the glass window. The full moon appeared enchanting, encircled by billows of her marijuana smoke. Light breeze kissed her face as crickets chirped to the stillness of the night.

Chapter 2

People Are Strange

People are strange when you're a stranger,
Faces look ugly when you're alone,
Women seem wicked when you're unwanted,
Streets are uneven when you're down.
—*Jim Morrison*

Layla sipped on her glass of water as she beckoned the turbaned waiter at the hotel's fancy coffee shop. Her hands seemed a little less shakier today as they held on to the tasselled menu. "Eggs and pancakes for me, please" ordered Jenna.

"Sausages and waffles for me, please" ordered Jovan.

"Just a cup of coffee for me, please, and that will be all. Thank you," said Layla with a smile as she handed the menu to the waiter, who bowed and left.

The morning sun was shining bright as its luminous rays entered through the window next to their table, which was clad in a white tablecloth, and shone on its silverware. Tiny specks drifted like diamonds in the slanted line of light that travelled through the curve of the tasselled window curtain and landed on the gleaming marble floor. Mirrored Rajasthani tapestry in bright colours hung from the walls. Carved ivory elephants, camels, and tigers looked at Jovan and Jenna as the two unfolded their crisply starched napkins and placed them on their laps, awaiting their breakfast.

Layla's blonde hair glimmered in bright sunlight as she sipped her coffee, lost in thought. Her eyes fell on her own reflection in the decorative, hand-carved mirror that hung across from her table. Golden locks fell on her fair yet tense face. The puffiness under her blue eyes had reduced but not vanished, even after a somewhat goodnight sleep. She fixed a hair pin inside her knot of hair that she had tied atop her head this morning. Her peach Lucknowi Chikan suit, an Indian outfit, was perfect for the hot day, keeping in mind that she had a five hours drive to Chandigarh after a visit to Tihar jail. These Lucknowi kurtis (long shirts) always came in handy for her jail visits. She had bought them in four colours from Khan Market: purple, pink, peach, and sky blue. Riccardo loved seeing her in Indian wear; he thought she looked like an Indian queen. Not that it mattered what Riccardo thought of her. There was never any love between the two. He was a huge mistake, and incorrigible too. Jovan was born out of this mistake. If it was not for the little guy, she would have snapped all ties with Riccardo long ago.

There was yet another reason she still met him: compassion. She felt bad for him, though she could not understand why. Why did she need to feel bad for a man who lived in luxury, even behind bars? He could afford phone service, television, and gourmet meals, and he could run a drug-trafficking racket from inside the jail. It was probably because she had a soft heart for humanity in general, and he *was* the father of her son. She had no better answer.

Layla fixed her kurti as she looked at her reflection in the tapestried mirror again. So he thought she looked like an Indian queen in Salwar kameez. *An Indian queen meeting her enslaved lover held in captivity?* She mused. *Huh!* A slight smirk broke at the corner of her lips.

"Mommy, I am done," said Jenna, breaking Layla out of her reverie.

"So am I," added Jovan.

Back in the hotel room, Jenna sat sprawled on the spacious armchair, fingering its decorative metal studs as she hesitatingly said, "Mommy, may I please come along? Please, pretty please?"

"No, Jenna darling. I am sorry. That place is not suitable for a pretty princess like you. It's filthy and disgusting. Jovan has no choice. He wants to see his dad, and his dad wants to see him. If it were in my hands, I would not take him there, but I am helpless," she said forcefully. "For you, I have ordered your favourite movie, *Sound of Music*. You lay back and enjoy the show, and we will be back in no time. Your Sohan Uncle is with you too. If you need something, let him know. Okey-dokey?"

"I want to see Uncle Riccardo too," Jenna whimpered, persisting.

"No, Jenna! Do not be so stubborn. You know how angry your grandparents, *Dadu* and *Dadi* ma, will be if they found out that you visited the jail with us. They will not allow you to spend your summer holidays with us in Poona anymore. Do you want that? They love you and want your very best. You do not want to offend them, do you?" asked Layla as she looked deeply in Jenna's big brown eyes.

"No," answered Jenna meekly with a downcast glance. "Okay, Mommy. I'll do as you say." She nodded and then rested her head helplessly on the soft back of the royal armchair as she pointed the remote control towards the TV, turning it on.

In order to calm her frayed nerves, Layla made a quick trip to the washroom for some powder comfort. Then she kissed Jenna goodbye and walked out the doorway, holding Jovan's hand and leaving Sohan Singh in charge. Standing by the roadside outside the hotel, Layla flagged down an auto rickshaw as she held Jovan's hand in a tight grip, trying to dodge the oncoming traffic.

A three-wheeler, coloured in green and yellow, *phut-phutted* towards them. "Where to madam?" asked the hurried driver in a muffled voice, looking askance into the enormously dilated pupils of Layla's blue eyes.

"To Tihar jail," Layla replied in a state of trance.

"Okay, madam. Sit," said the driver as he squirted red spit out of his mouth, exposing his stained teeth dyed crimson, probably from years of chewing on tobacco-filled betel leaves. Jovan side-stepped to avoid the flying spit and hopped inside the three-wheeler, sitting on the thinly cushioned metal passenger seat. The driver bent over, and with his left hand, he grasped a lever attached to the bottom and jerked it upwards. The tiny engine came to life, and they *phut-phutted* their way into the maddening traffic, leaving behind a trail of dust. With every pothole, they jerked their necks and leaped inches into the air, Layla's head almost touching the yellow plastic hood of the auto rickshaw. Jovan giggled, and Layla smiled. The ride was not the least bit comfortable, but it was satisfactory. Layla was not in the habit of bringing any belonging of the Sandhu family with her when she went to see Riccardo, be it Jenna or their chauffeured black Mercedes.

Soon they jolted in front of a huge compound, encircled by a high wall mounted with barbed-wire fence. Guns stuck out from the corner towers. This was Tihar jail, the largest complex of high-security prisons in all of South Asia. The two clambered out of the auto rickshaw holding their stiff necks, and they walked alongside the beige wall and past the gigantic metal gate towards the *mulakat* (meet-up) chamber of Jail Two. A handcuffed inmate walked out of the minuscule metal door built inside the gargantuan metal gate, encircled by seven to eight policemen dressed in khaki uniforms. The prisoner stared at Jovan as he walked past him. Jovan looked away nervously.

"*Chal chal jaldi kar, aage dekh bhai* (Move fast, look forward)," yelled a ferocious-looking policeman with a huge mole under his eye and an overgrown Air India maharaja moustache. He inhumanely shoved the prisoner into the red-striped blue police van that read, "Delhi Police."

Jovan clutched onto his mommy's arm, hiding his face in it.

"What happened? Are you scared of the prisoner, honey?" asked Layla, caressing Jovan's hair as he walked along with shaky legs.

"No, Mommy," answered Jovan in a whisper.

"Then are you scared of the policemen?"

"Maybe ... Um, I think so. I don't know," he answered softly, lifting his head up and looking at her with helpless blue eyes. A blob of sweat ran down his tiny, confused, and wrinkled forehead.

Layla knelt down and placed her hand lovingly on Jovan's glistening red cheek, looking deep into his eyes. "Boy, oh boy!" she whispered softly as she hugged him dearly for a moment. Then she opened up a bottle of cold Bisleri water and put the mouth on Jovan's dry, chapped lips. Water cascaded off the side of his cheek and neck, and inside his T-shirt, as he gulped it down.

The stench of urine emanated from the corners of the walls on the outside of the meeting chamber. Flies buzzed over an overfilled garbage can placed in a corner as the two walked inside a hall crammed with loud people. Distressed people pressed against them as they worked their way towards a corner bench. Layla seated Jovan on a metal bench, and then she pushed and shoved her way into the office to book a meeting with Riccardo. Jovan sat stiffly with his handkerchief placed against his nose in order to avoid breathing in too much of the sweaty, urine-laced air. Even so, he could distinctly smell the metallic stink of the steel bench on his hand.

Jovan felt uneasy in a hall overcrowded with people rubbing and brushing against each other's sweaty bodies. Everyone was shouting at someone. A child cried, a mother yelled, and an old man sat in a corner with his head cupped in his hands, looking defeated. A woman slapped the flat of her hand against her forehead as she wailed. Jovan cringed on the inside and tried to distract himself from his surroundings by thinking about what Jenna would be doing at this moment. He imagined her sitting in her nice, fancy hotel room on her royal armchair with her feet placed on the futon, watching *Sound of Music*. She was probably singing along with Julie Andrews.

> Raindrops on roses and whiskers on kittens,
>
> Bright copper kettles and warm woollen mittens,
>
> Brown paper packages tied up with strings,
>
> These are a few of my favourite things.

Jovan was humming these lines softly with closed eyes, oblivious of his surroundings, when Layla walked over to him and gently tapped him on the shoulder, "We've got over an hour to pass before we see Dad, hon. Let's go to the department store and the fruit shop. Come on." Jovan sprung up on his feet and walked cautiously towards the door, holding on to Layla's hand. Touching anything in the hall creeped him out. He avoided accidentally brushing against layers of crud on the walls.

After another short and bumpy auto rickshaw ride, they walked inside a store with a rusted store sign that read, "New York Department Store." Jovan wondered why it was named after New York when it was located in Delhi. He had seen many of these signs: "London drycleaners." "German Bakery." "Paris Jewellers." When questioned, Mommy answered that it was called "New York Department Store" probably because it carried imported stuff that was not manufactured in India. Was all the stuff manufactured in New York, then? Mommy answered no. Jovan was confused.

Layla bought a pack of Dove soap, two large bottles of Revlon shampoo and conditioner, Axe deodorant, and a bottle of Old Spice aftershave. After Layla paid the bill, the shopkeeper behind the counter, who had droopy eyes and a bored look on his face, gave her a few Cadbury chocolate éclairs instead of change. Jovan grabbed them with a wide smile.

Next they walked inside Gulshan Fruit Juice, a shop that sold fruit, freshly squeezed fruit juice, lemonade, and a drink made of yogurt called lassi. Layla and Jovan sat on the wobbly plastic chairs inside the little shack. Layla waved a fly away from her glass as she sipped on mixed fruit juice, and Jovan guzzled down his favourite drink of mango lassi. Layla then bought some mangoes, lychees, papaya, and grapes and got them neatly packed in bags.

After another short and bumpy auto rickshaw ride, they were back in the meeting chamber of Jail Two. It was 1:00 p.m. and time to see Riccardo. Jovan was happy that they were not meeting Daddy the ordinary way that all other prisoners met their kith and kin. He had seen Mommy grease some greedy palms, and sleazy policemen with wide grins then ushered them inside a small meeting room. On the left were people standing on either sides of three sets of iron bars. Inmates stood on the inner side of the thick sets of bars, and visitors were on the outer side. People leaned and pressed on one another as they yelled to be heard. Some 40 to 50 people shouting at the same time created a chaotic medley. Jovan plugged his ears as he walked past them.

"Daddy!" screamed Jovan joyously as he saw Riccardo waiting inside a Lilliputian room. The boy ran into his open arms as the two hugged. Layla left the fruit and toiletries with the policemen, who after screening them would forward those to Riccardo.

"I am so happy to see you, Son," said Riccardo in his loud, musical Italian accent as he kissed and tightly hugged Jovan. "You have grown taller, and you have started looking so much like your mommy." Riccardo kneeled on the floor and shuffled Jovan's hair lovingly. Jovan smiled with twinkling eyes.

Riccardo was a medium-statured man with shoulder length sandy brown silky hair and a well-built torso. He seemingly hid deep, dark secrets in his ocean-blue eyes. Riccardo walked over to Layla and hugged her. "You don't look very well, *amore mio*. What happened?" he said with a look of concern.

"Hmm, I am okay, Ricco. Just a bit stressed, nervous," she moaned.

"But why?" he asked as he seated Jovan on a plastic chair in a corner and gave him a pen and a paper, asking him to sketch something he liked. The two adults seated themselves on a steel bench in the other corner of the room next to one another. Layla discreetly took out a wad of 500-rupee notes and slipped them into Riccardo's pocket.

"*Grazie, amore mio,*" he whispered as he gave her a peck on the lips. "I am worried, though. Why do you look so weak, Bella? Are you doing too much coke?" Riccardo had a concerned look on his face as he wrapped his arm around Layla's shoulder. He continued after a pause. "I am asking because I am worried about you."

The question angered Layla. "You needn't be worried, Riccardo. It's none of your business what I do and what I don't. And please don't try to involve me in *your* business," she retorted, burning with fury as she flung his arm away from her shoulder and gave him an angry look.

"What do you mean, love?" questioned Riccardo with a frown as he brought the fingertips of his right hand together and moved it up and down frantically, in Italian fashion.

"Leonardo said that you want me to carry a heroin-stacked suitcase to Chandigarh, to Jenna's grandparents' house—to my in-laws' house. I have children, Riccardo. Keep me out of this mess." She lashed out at him ferociously.

"It is just because Monika isn't available for a few days, and Leonardo is leaving for Milano tonight. Please don't jeopardize the situation, Layla. What I earn is for you and Jovan, isn't it, love? Moreover, once I am released, I will not be doing this. I will earn by honest means, and we can live as a happy family in Roma. You, me, Jenna, and Jovan," said Riccardo with a pitiful face.

Layla looked at him suspiciously. She knew that old habits die hard. To her, he appeared like a wolf in sheep's clothing. Nevertheless, she felt helpless and vulnerable, like a sheep caught in a tiger's trap. Jovan's sweet face, his love for his father, and his desire for a happy family melted Layla. Maybe, just maybe, Riccardo would change. Maybe he was not lying. A faint hope flickered in her heart. She felt as if she had no choice at this point in her life but to hope against hope and give in. Layla deflated. "Okay, but it's the very last time, Ricco," she mumbled weakly.

"I love you, *amore mio*." He kissed her and hugged her tight.

A policeman, with bulging black eyes strode towards the small meeting room and hit his baton on the door. "Time over," he said in a rude, authoritative voice.

"Two minutes more?" requested Riccardo, slyly shoving a crisp 500-rupee note down the man's pocket.

"Okay, but only two minutes and no more," instructed the policeman as he raised one eyebrow, pointed his baton at Riccardo, and then left with a smug smile.

"Let us see what my son has sketched," said Riccardo. He walked over to Jovan, knelt down, and turned around the paper that Jovan had been sketching on.

Jovan had chosen to sketch a happy family holding hands. "This is you, Mommy, Jenna, and me walking by a stream in a park." He smiled his missing-tooth smile as he pointed to the figures he had been sketching. Layla's eyes welled up with tears.

"The park is in Roma, is it?" asked Riccardo.

"Maybe, Daddy," answered Jovan with a smile. Riccardo hugged Layla and Jovan. Layla finally dropped her armour and gave in with a bit of reluctance.

After a few more kisses and hugs, Layla and Jovan bid farewell to Riccardo. They went *phut-phutting* their way back to the hotel Taj Palace.

Jovan was happy to be back in his hotel room. After a late lunch of pasta with garlic bread, ordered through room service, Jenna and Jovan played Snakes and Ladders while sprawled on bed. Jenna propped herself on an elbow as she lay sideways and threw the dice. "Yay! I win!" she shouted excitedly.

Layla shambled over to Leonardo's room, lost in worrisome thoughts. "Here you come, Bella. I was eagerly waiting for you." He welcomed her with a kiss on her cheek.

"I give in, Leo. Where is the suitcase?"

"Here it is, Bella. It has 5 kilograms of heroin, separately packed in 26 small bags, sealed inside its fake bottom. On the inside, simply pack your clothes." He smiled mischievously. "Monika will contact you and will pick it up from you in a few days."

"Hmm ... all right," answered Layla.

"Care for a line or two?"

"Sure."

Leo chopped some cocaine and offered it to Layla in neatly organized lines decorated on a gilded mirror. She leaned forward and snorted a line. "Boy, oh boy!" she mumbled in relief as she gently moved a golden strand of hair off her forehead and sunk back in her chair with closed eyes. A sniff of cocaine brought tranquillity to her troubled mind. As the powder started relaxing her limbs, she leaned farther back, letting her body melt in the cushy chair and revelling in the ecstatic feeling of warmth and comfort coursing through her body. Suddenly, all seemed perfect and powdery beautiful.

Chapter 3
Strange Days

Strange days have found us,
Strange days have tracked us down,
They are going to destroy our casual joys,
We shall go on playing or find a new town.

—*Jim Morrison*

Sohan Singh loaded the baggage into the trunk of the shining black Mercedes while Layla, Jenna, and Jovan flopped on the back seat. Layla slid the heroin-filled suitcase under the driver's seat by her feet and tilted back her weary head. She dozed off in no time as they drove towards Chandigarh.

Jovan and Jenna peered out of the car window. The streets were full of three-wheelers, rickshaws, motorbikes, scooters, cars, and truck, all blasting their horns. Due to the overcrowded roads, the Mercedes was moving at a snail's pace. As Jenna looked out of the left side of the car window, she witnessed an adjacent truck hit the rear end of a Fiat ahead of it. The truck driver yelled at the driver of the Fiat for braking too fast. The car driver yelled back, saying he needed to keep distance. Onlookers enjoyed the show, some siding with the truck driver and some with the car driver. The hurling of curses and swears at one another caused a traffic jam, and the traffic did not budge for almost 15 minutes. Finally, once the dispute was settled, the traffic crawled slowly. It took Sohan Singh forever to drive out of the metropolis and onto the Delhi Chandigarh highway.

It was 4:00 p.m., and it seemed like they were now going to race headlong into the evening. Sohan Singh slithered with expertise through hordes of colourful trucks and lorries with roaring engines and exhaust pipes that emitted fat clouds of dark-grey smoke. The air conditioning in the car was cranked to the maximum, and the windows were rolled up in order to be saved from the atmospheric pollution.

As they drove, Jenna and Jovan enjoyed the road show. All the trucks had their metallic outer bodies painted with colourful artwork like peacocks, flowers, and amusing slogans. Many trucks had a black shoe dangling at the rear end and others had a scary face with wide eyes and a tongue hanging out. This was in order to be saved from the evil eye, Sohan Singh had explained. Almost all the trucks on road had one common saying written at their rear end: *"Buri nazar waale tera muh kaala,"* meaning "The one with the evil eye, your face is black." Often *nimbu mirchi* (lemon and chilli) hung alongside it. Jenna and Jovan did not like this saying and believed that it should be banned because it promoted racism. Layla strongly believed the same. Jenna had even written a letter to the prime minister of India, requesting him to ban the saying nationwide. Jenna and Jovan undoubtedly believed he would soon take action.

Jenna and Jovan enjoyed looking at the colourful roadside restaurants on either sides of the highway, known as *dhabas*. They played a game of who could count more *dhabas*. The names of a *dhaba*, once taken, could not to be repeated. "That's *Saini da dhaba*," said Jenna.

"That's *Pehalwan da Dhaba*," said Jovan.

"That's *Giani da dhaba,*" said Jenna. Jovan was leading because he had more dhabas on his side.

Halfway through, as they hit Karnal, a small town between Delhi and Chandigarh, it was time for a chai break. Sohan Singh chose the *Sher-e-Punjab* dhaba to drink his masala chai. Loud Bollywood music blared from the speakers at the dhaba as Sohan Singh parked the shining black Mercedes besides a colourful truck. Layla was still fast asleep.

"Do you want to eat or drink something, children?" asked Sohan Singh.

"Thumbs-up for me, please," requested Jovan.

"Coca-Cola for me, please." said Jenna. "Why do you always drink Thumbs-up, Jovan? Try Coca-Cola for once."

"No, thank you. Coca-cola is too mild for me. I like the strong, fizzy taste of Thumbs-up. Thumbs-up is not for the faint of heart, you see." He teased Jenna as he giggled. She scrunched her face, threw him a nasty look, and then turned away.

"Sohan Uncle, I also need to pee," Jovan called after Sohan Singh, who was walking towards the dhaba.

"Okay, *kaka ji* (young lad). Come along with me," said Sohan Singh as he extended his hand and helped Jovan hop out of the car. They walked past clusters of people sitting on jute beds enjoying masala chai, and others were around plastic tables relishing spicy Indian cuisine. Sohan Singh and Jovan wended down a gravel path towards the back of the dhaba, where there were two metal doors with rusty streaks on them. One read "Gents Latrine," and the other said "Ladies Latrine." Jovan walked inside the one for gents, but he was out in no time with his handkerchief placed on his nose.

"No, Sohan Uncle. I can't use this. Is there another option?" Sohan Singh looked towards the outside wall of the dhaba, against which a man was urinating. Jovan shook his head dismissively "No! Not there either." Jovan finally chose to piddle in the open field behind the dhaba while Sohan Singh stood guard.

Once relieved, Jovan was back in the car sipping on his Thumbs-up. "Thumbs-up! Taste the thunder!" He sang the jingle as he enjoyed his chilled, super-fizzy drink, nudging Jenna, who smugly quaffed her Coca Cola. Sohan Singh smiled while watching the two as he sipped on his super sweet, super warm and super spicy masala chai. After the customary returning of the bottles, they were back on the road.

"Now we are crossing the city of Kurukshetra, children. Do you know what it is famous for?" said Sohan Singh.

"Of course! The Kurukshetra war of the Mahabharata was fought here, and it is the birth place of the Holy Bhagavad Gita, the holy book of the Hindus. Lord Krishna preached Bhagavad Gita to Arjuna on this land when Arjuna was in a dilemma," answered Jenna with a sense of pride.

"Very good, Jenna! How do you know this?" said Sohan Singh, seeming a bit startled as he looked at Jenna in the rear-view mirror.

"Mommy listens to the Bhagavad Gita summary and plays it at home. We overhear it too. Mommy meditates a lot, you know" she answered.

"Yes, I know Layla Madam meditates. Can you kids tell me one lesson of the Bhagavad Gita?"

"Whatever happened, happened for the good. Whatever is happening, is happening for the good. Whatever will happen, will also happen for the good." Jovan and Jenna recited the lines like poetry, with cheerful smiles and hopeful eyes.

"Very good, children! You are wise. In simple words, many times unpleasant things happen in life, and we fail to understand why they happen. We feel hurt and sad in that moment. Our shortcoming as human beings is that we fail to see the divine plan behind it, or the big picture. Always trust the universe and existence because it has a good plan in place for you. You may not be able to see it right now, but in the end, only something good comes out of everything. So always trust!"

"Okay, Sohan Uncle! Thank you for explaining so well," said Jenna with a smile.

"Could we please play some music now?" requested Jovan.

"Layla Madam is fast asleep. What if she wakes up, *kaka ji*?"

"No, she never wakes up when she is fast asleep," argued Jenna.

"Please, Uncle. Pick up that cassette lying there that says Wham, and insert it in, please."

Sohan Singh did so. Jenna and Jovan sang and danced along with the songs as they jerked their shoulders and snapped their fingers. "Wake me up before you go-go. Don't leave me hanging on like a yo-yo ..."

After exhausting all their energy, they slept for the rest of the ride to Chandigarh.

"Layla Madam ji, we are almost home," called out Sohan Singh in an attempt to wake up Layla.

Jovan heard Sohan Singh call out and woke up abruptly, rubbing his eyes eagerly. "Mommy, Mommy, wake up. We are almost home," he said joyously while he shook Layla. "Wake up, Jenna. We are in Chandigarh," he said ecstatically, as he jolted Jenna. "I am so excited to see Wolfie! Oh, how I can't wait," he said, impatiently rubbing his hands together.

Jovan was more excited to see Wolfie, his little West Highland terrier, than anybody else in the house. Urvashi, Layla's German *sannyasin* friend in Poona, had left for Germany for good, and she had left the little dog with Layla and Jovan two years back. The dog was only four months old then and had taken an immediate liking to Jovan. Jovan had changed his name from Pluto to Wolfie; he said that he found Wolfie cuter. Mommy also explained the logic behind the name. She told Jovan that when he was in his mommy's tummy, Mommy used to listen to a lot of Mozart symphonies, and Jovan kicked a lot when Mozart music played. That was probably an indication that he felt very happy listening to Mozart's music. Wolfie could be considered the short form for Amadeus Wolfgang Mozart. It was a name Jovan had formed a connection with before being born. Jovan felt very happy about the fact and loved the explanation behind his dog's name.

Jenna and Jovan shared Wolfie, and they both loved him. The problem was that Jenna lived with her paternal grandparents in Chandigarh and visited Layla and Jovan only during holidays, whereas Jovan lived with mommy in Poona. Half of the time Wolfie lived in Poona, and half of the time he was in Chandigarh. This year when Jenna left for Poona to spend summer holidays with Layla and Jovan, she couldn't take Wolfie along because he wasn't feeling very well, and Wolfie's doctor lived in Chandigarh. No question arose of taking a chance with Wolfie's health, so he was left behind in Dadu, Dadi Ma, and Bali Ram's care.

"Jenna, wake up. Mommy, wake up!" Jovan shook Layla and Jenna again. Both woke up, rubbing their eyes slowly. Jovan and Jenna looked eagerly out of the car window. They recognized the landmarks: a sign saying "Welcome to Chandigarh—The City Beautiful," the *Tribune* building (leading newspaper of India) with its daily headlines flashing, and the Gurudwara (Sikh temple) with its orange flag standing tall. Jovan and Jenna exchanged warm smiles, knowing that their destination was minutes away.

The black Mercedes cruised through the wide roads lined with lush green trees on both sides, and then it looped around circular roundabouts. The almost empty roads were a marked contrast from Delhi's overcrowded roads causing endless traffic jams. Past the golf club and the lake, they were now in Sector Two, where Jenna's paternal grandparents lived.

It was 7:30 p.m., and the blazing sun was slipping behind the tall Ashoka trees that lined the street leading towards the Sandhu mansion. A majestic black metal arched gate stood in all its splendour with tall, brightly lit lampposts on either side. On the right hand side of the gate hung a decorative bronze name plate with light reflecting on it: "The Sandhus." Sohan Singh honked the horn, and Kashi Ram, the gardener, came running and opened the gate wide.

"Ram Ram (Hello), Madam ji. Ram Ram, Kaka ji, and Baby ji," greeted Kashi Ram with enthusiasm, holding the gate from inside while Sohan Singh drove over the fancy cobblestone driveway lined with palm trees and garden lanterns. Green palms swayed against the dark-blue sky in the warm breeze. The sprawling green lawn was adorned with a beautiful, hand-carved marble cherub estate garden fountain that had soothing water flowing from all sides. Marigolds, petunias, zinnias, carnations, and lilies bloomed in all colours. Bright-pink bougainvillea wrapped around the fence on either sides of the house. Tree leaves rustled and birds chirped. Crows cawed from their perches on the branches of jackfruit and mango trees that lined the backyard of the house. This was Dadi ma's favourite part of the house because she made jams, jelly, pickles, and chutney from the fruits of these trees.

Jovan and Jenna hopped out of the Mercedes and ran towards miniature white marble pillars that lined the short fleet of stairs leading to the main entrance of a large, wooden double door with shiny brass handles. Before Bali Ram could fully open the door, white and fluffy Wolfie squeezed out and almost jumped out of his skin to greet Jovan and Jenna. He ran hysterically from Jenna to Jovan and back again, putting his paws all over them. Layla clambered slowly out of the car with a lengthy shadow following behind her. Wolfie ran towards her with great alacrity and soon was all over her as she knelt down. Layla beamed with joy, forgetting all her woes for a few moments as she petted him generously and carried him in her lap towards the main door.

"Dadu! Dadi ma!" shouted Jenna with excitement as she saw her grandparents walking out of the main door. She ran into their open arms. Jovan plodded a bit slowly and reluctantly behind Jenna.

"My sweetheart! Here you are!" said Dadu cheerfully as he picked up Jenna in his arms and kissed her lovingly.

"We missed you so much, Darling," said Dadi ma, taking her turn to enthusiastically kiss and hug Jenna.

"Come here, Jovan. Give us a hug!" said Dadu with a smile as he moved towards Jovan and held him in his arms. Dadi ma did the same thing nonchalantly.

"Sat Sri Akal, Papa and Mamma," said Layla respectfully as she bent and touched their feet. She was accustomed to greeting her in-laws in the traditional Indian way because that was how her late husband, Gary, and she had greeted them as a couple. Those were the good old days, when Gary was alive.

"Sat Sri Akal, beta ji (child)," said Papa and Mamma as they blessed and hugged her before walking inside.

A huge crystal chandelier hung from the ceiling of the grand living room, which was embellished with brass elephants and horses in its corners. Stuffed animals were mounted on walls for display as hunting trophies. Beneath a leopard skin that adorned the main wall of the majestic living room hung a huge brass framed portrait of Gary. He stood tall in his horse riding gear—his beige Jodhpurs, breeches, riding boots, and gloves—as he placed his hand on his favourite steed, Top Gun. Gary, with his outstanding looks, big brown eyes, sharp nose, and a chiselled jawline, looked like a dashing Indian prince. Layla fondly remembered painting this portrait of Gary in Goa a few days after he had just won a polo tournament.

How he had loved the painting! "You work magic with your brush strokes, Layla," he had told her numerous times.

"Layla, beta ji, please freshen up. Let's have a drink together. The dinner will be laid at 8:40 p.m. sharp," instructed Jenna's grandfather, better known as Brigadier Amrinder Singh Sandhu. He was a tall and well-built Sikh with a trimmed beard and a charming personality. Dadu was a strict disciplinarian regarding daily routines, having spent over 35 years in the service of the Indian Army. He was of a jovial and loving nature just as long as no daily rules were broken. Everyone in the house needed to follow a strict timeline. There was a set time for waking up and a set time for a morning jog by the *Sukhna* Lake. He had a set time for breakfast, lunch, siesta, evening walk, and even evening scotch. He consumed two standard drinks of scotch on the rocks from 7:30–8:30 p.m., followed by dinner at 8:40 p.m. Layla was the exact opposite and followed no timelines at all, but they still shared a great relationship. Layla made sure though that when she visited the Sandhu house, she followed all their timelines out of respect. Her visits never extended more than a few days, though.

"Jenna! You go to your room, please, and freshen up before dinner is laid. Bimla! You please look after Jenna. Jovan! You go with your mommy and get fresh. Sohan Singh! Please place the baggage in their respective rooms," instructed Dadi ma, authoritatively pointing her finger towards each person whom she addressed. Dadi ma, also known as Harinder Kaur Sandhu, was a beautiful and spiffy woman with fair skin, green eyes, and a roman nose. She had two major passions in life, cooking and socialising. She doted on Jenna but was not particularly fond of Jovan, for obvious reasons. When people in her social circle gossiped about Jovan and his father, she would march home, fuming with anger, and she would narrate her tales of woe to Dadu, who would calm her down with a glass of scotch.

Jenna walked up the gleaming spiral staircase that led to her room with Bimla, her ayah (caretaker), walking behind her for assistance. Layla walked into her room on the ground floor with large bay window that opened up to the front garden.

"Madam ji, here are the suitcases," said Sohan Singh as he placed the luggage in Layla's room.

"There was also one small black leather suitcase that I placed by my feet in front. It must have slipped under your seat. Could you bring that one in too, please?" requested Layla after quickly browsing through the luggage.

Sohan Singh was back in a jiffy with the heroin-filled suitcase and plopped it down. "Anything else, Madam ji?" asked Sohan Singh, wiping the sweat that poured from his temples with a handkerchief.

"No, thank you, Sohan Singh. That'll be all," said Layla. After Sohan Singh left the room, Layla quickly slid the heroin suitcase on the top shelf of her armoire, placing her clothes over and around it to keep it hidden from view. She couldn't wait for Monika to pick it up from her. "Damn Riccardo!" she cursed in frustration, realising what he was making her do.

After freshening up, Dadu, Dadi ma, and Layla sat in the front garden on wicker chairs while Bali Ram served scotch and soda to the ladies and scotch on the rocks to Dadu, along with some roasted peanuts and fresh fruit salad on the side. Jenna and Jovan played fetch with Wolfie, who barked with excitement as he ran behind the tennis ball. The sky had turned a pinkish grey, and the three adults enjoyed the splendour of the fading light as they sipped on their drinks. The garden lights were switched on as the sky turned darker.

Over their drinks, Dadu and Dadi ma talked about the importance of a healthy lifestyle, good nutrition, exercise, and education for the children. Layla nodded mechanically for most of the conversation till a big fruit bat dived down to her neck and scared her out of her seat. Dadu leaped towards the bat, grabbed it by its end, and flung it away. It was quite a show for the kids: shriek, jump, and rescue. They loved it.

"The table is laid," said Bali Ram as he glided out of the main door. They walked in and sat around a grand, eight-chair mahogany dining table. Layla fidgeted around with her fork and spoon, nibbling a bit while the others enjoyed a sumptuous meal. After finishing up, Layla, Jenna, and Jovan kissed Dadu and Dadi ma goodnight and were off to their respective rooms. After putting Jovan to bed, Layla sniffed a few lines of heroin in the bathroom. Her body and mind eased as the brownish powder seeped into her body. She then took a long, warm bath in the tub to ease her aching calves. These few hours of greetings and polite conversations had been nerve-racking for her.

After the warm bath, she popped a few pills of Valium, sank deep into her bed, and stared blankly at the ceiling, mulling over her predicament in life. Though the drug relaxed her body and mind, it had become a medical necessity for her survival. How she loathed her dependence on drugs. She was sick of her addiction and was determined to get clean. She had already contacted a rehabilitation centre in New York and had booked herself in for an eight-week clean-up program. She was keenly looking forward to it in the coming month. Lost in thought, Layla gradually fell asleep, smelling in the fragrance of jasmine that wafted through the large window she had left partly open.

It was 4:00 a.m. when the doorbell rang. Bali Ram woke up a bit startled, wondering who could be at the gate at this early an hour. He clumsily drew aside the mosquito net wrapped around his bed, rubbed his sleepy eyes, tottered out of the bed, and dragged himself to the gate. The night was still, and nothing could be heard except the barking of a distant dog and the loud, constant chirping of male crickets trying to attract mates. As Bali Ram clang opened the main gate, a form of a man, covered in a blanket with just his eyes showing, emerged from the darkness.

"Is Layla Madam at home?" the man inquired in a muffled voice.

"Yes, but who are you?" mumbled Bali Ram, appearing a bit confused and dazed.

"Action!" yelled the man loudly, throwing aside his blanket and revealing his police uniform. Suddenly some 20 policemen emerged from under the bushes, armed with guns. They had surrounded the house from all four sides. Bali Ram's knees shook as he trembled with fear.

A horde of policemen strode into the house. Lights turned on, and everyone woke up. Two female police officers stormed inside Layla's room, followed by male officers. "What's the matter?" yelled Layla in a voice dripping with fear.

"We have information that you have five kilograms of heroin on you," said the chief police officer in a grating voice. The officer, who sported a Zapata moustache and chewed on a wad of tobacco, glared lecherously at Layla, who nervously wrapped a gown around her nightie with shaky hands. The top buttons of his uniform shirt were open, and a tuft of black chest hair stuck out as he stared and smirked at her.

"Please show me your passport," ordered the officer as the other policemen searched the room, looking into nooks and corners. Dadu and Dadi ma rushed down. Dadu agitatedly took the chief officer aside to ask what was going on, and Dadi ma stood by the door side with a look of horror on her pale face.

"What's the matter, Officer? Why are you in my house? I am a respectable man. I have served the Indian Army for over 35 years. Stop this nonsense at once!" commanded Dadu in an aggravated tone.

"I understand, Brigadier Sahib. I know that you are a respectable man. But Ms. Layla, who unfortunately happens to be your late son's wife, is a dangerous criminal," stated the police officer, raising an eyebrow and widening his bulging black eyes. "She is a drug dealer and a drug addict. She has been Riccardo's accomplice and partner in crime for past seven years. You know Riccardo—the criminal who runs a huge drug trafficking racket, supplying hash and heroin to Western countries. Three of his gang members were caught yesterday, and they employ the same modus operandi. Stashes of heroine are sealed inside the fake bottoms of custom-made suitcases. A female gang member, Monika, was caught yesterday, and she revealed that she was going to pick up a suitcase filled with five kilograms of heroin from Ms. Layla. Have patience, Brigadier Sahib. All will be crystal-clear once we recover the suitcase," the chief police officer explained slowly and calmly.

"And if no suitcase is found, this will be your last day in office," threatened Dadu.

"Relax, Brigadier Sahib! And who is this little boy on the bed? He is Riccardo's son, right?" The sleazy police officer lowered an eyebrow and pointed his baton towards Jovan with his gold-laden wrist and fingers.

"Mind your own business, Officer," shouted Dadu.

"That's exactly what I am doing, Brigadier Sahib," jeered the officer.

Jovan sat on the bed with a shocked look on his face, unaware of what was going on. All he knew was that the ugly, cruel policemen had invaded his world, and he intuitively feared that they were going to take away from him everything that was precious to him: his smile, his laughter, his love, his happiness, his world. His thin body trembled like a leaf, sensing a disaster.

Jenna tip-toed behind Dadi ma, frightened and scared. Dadi ma pressed Jenna's face protectively against her chest as she called out to Bimla. "Bimla, take the children to the upstairs room and distract them somehow," she instructed sternly as she ushered them both out of the room.

"I found some heroin powder on the bathroom shelf," said one police officer gleefully as he ran out of the bathroom door with a look of victory. Dadu, Dadi ma, and the house staff stood still; they were stunned, shocked and horrified.

The chief officer, who was leafing through the pages of Layla's passport, didn't look up. "Search more. First this room, then the rest of the house." Policemen turned the room upside down as they poked into drawers and shelves, rummaged through the wardrobe, and threw all clothes on the bed.

"Here is the suitcase! It's similar to the ones recovered yesterday," stated an overenthusiastic policeman, holding up the leather suitcase like a trophy.

"Rip it open" ordered the chief officer. With knives and scissors, they stabbed, ripped, and tore apart the leather. Scraps of leather flew all over, and a police officer held stashes of heroin in his hand. "You are under arrest! I will have to manacle you, Ms. Layla" said the chief officer as he handcuffed her and walked her out of the house.

"There must be some mistake!" persisted Dadu, sounding a bit nervous and unsure this time.

"No, there is no mistake, Brigadier Sahib. Please wake up to reality now," said the chief officer as he placed his reassuring hands on Dadu's defeated shoulders.

Sandhu family and staff stood aghast and thunderstruck. They were still bewildered as Layla was walked out of the door in handcuffs. Layla doddered unsteadily towards the gate as Jenna and Jovan peered from the window of their room with hands curled around their eyes. Tears rolled down their rosy cheeks as they watched their mother getting pushed into a canvas-covered Jeep. A red-striped police van followed her into the dark unknown, leaving behind a trail of dust.

Chapter 4

THIS IS THE END

This is the end, beautiful friend.
This is the end, my only friend, the end,
Of our elaborate plans, the end,
Of everything that stands, the end.
No safety or surprise, the end.
I'll never look into your eyes again . . .
— *Jim Morrison*

20 years later, 2005

The June night was dark, still, and hot. The old ceiling fan rotated slowly, making a creaky sound and stirring the top strands of Layla's hair as she lay half asleep on the pallet-covered concrete floor of her cell, tossing and turning. She was beginning to feel uneasy. First she felt a slight heartburn, and then she felt a tightness around her chest. The uneasiness increased, and soon she found herself sweating, panting, and gasping for breath as the tightness spread to her arms, neck, jaw, and back. She huffed and puffed with her fingers clenched against her chest, but she was unable to speak or call out.

Fear gripped her, and hundreds of thoughts flooded her mind simultaneously. Were these going to be the last few moments of her life? Was she not destined to be released from this prison that she had entered 20 years back? Was she never going to see Jovan and Jenna again?

The pain increased, causing Layla to close her eyes in surrender. As she did so, an image of Lord Krishna appeared in her mind's eye, narrating the holy lines of Bhagavad Gita that she had read every morning at dawn for past 20 years.

> That which is born shall die, but the *Atman* (soul) is neither born nor shall it die. Then what is the reason to be sad? The body is transient, but the soul is deathless and indivisible. The *Atman* is unborn, eternal, changeless, and inexhaustible. Just as a man casts off worn out clothes and puts on new ones, so also the *Atman* casts off worn out bodies, and enters others which are new. Why do you worry without cause? Whom do you fear without reason? Who can kill you? What did you lose that you cry about? What did you bring with you that you think you have lost? You did not bring anything—whatever you have, you received from here. Whatever you have given, you have given only here. You came empty-handed, and you will leave empty-handed.

Having said these lines, the image of Lord Krishna vanished.

The storm in Layla's mind calmed down. The waters lay still. A little girl's voice echoed in the distance. "Mother, Mother! Find me! I am here."

Layla opened her eyes abruptly. She had read and heard that a person's whole life flashes before her mind's eye before breathing her last breath. The voice grew louder. "Mother, I am here!" Layla gently closed her eyes and gave in as she followed the voice.

"Mother! Find me!"

"Where are you, my little princess? I am coming to find you. Are you under the table?"

"No ..."

"Are you behind the door?"

"No."

"Are you behind the Christmas tree? I see you now, and I am going to get you!" said Doreen, Layla's mother, as she ran behind the little girl, who slinked from behind the lit Christmas tree wearing a red and green checked frock, along with red bows in her golden hair. Little Layla giggled and chuckled as she scurried around the furniture on her 30th-floor penthouse perched on top of her father's grand hotel, the York, situated in downtown Manhattan.

"Got you, my lovely, and now it's bedtime!" exclaimed Doreen with a warm smile as she grabbed Layla in a hug and kissed her. "Valerie, please get Layla changed into her night dress, and I will put her to sleep."

"Yes, Ma'am," answered Valerie, the governess. She walked Layla to her room.

Layla's bedroom faced other skyscrapers on Fifth Avenue. She looked outside the bay window of her bedroom as she sat snuggled up in her white canopy covered bed, wearing her pretty pink laced nightie. Snowflakes fell from the sky like sparkling white diamonds on buildings, and trees lit up with bright Christmas lights. A distant singing of Christmas carols could be heard as Valerie cracked opened the window a little, letting in cold, crisp, and fresh air.

"Thank you for changing her, Valerie. You can retire to your room now. Have a good night!" said Doreen as she curled up next to Layla on the bed and gave her daughter a mug of peppermint white hot chocolate.

"Goodnight, Ma'am" said Valerie as she walked out of the doorway.

"What would you like me to read to you tonight, Darling?" asked Doreen caressing Layla's soft hair as she sipped on her warm and sweet milk.

"Could you please read to me *The Life and Adventures of Santa Claus?*" requested Layla.

"Sure, Darling," said Doreen. She started reading the story while gently stroking Layla's hair. In no time, Layla fell fast asleep in her mother's warm, secure arms. Doreen softly tucked her in the bed and kissed her goodnight.

As a little girl, Layla had lived the coddled life of an American princess. She was born to David and Doreen Smith on the night of January 10, 1949, in Bellevue Hospital Center, Manhattan. Her father was a successful hotelier, and her mother was a thorough socialite who was knee-deep into diamonds and fashion. Layla grew up speaking French with her Parisian nanny, took ballet and piano lessons, and went to a high-end, all-girls school in her chauffeured pink Cadillac.

As the years rolled by, Layla's father got too busy making money, and her mother got too busy socialising. As a result, Layla started spending most of her time in her friend Belinda's company. Life was beautiful with Belinda who lived in a building across from hers. Their friendship began when they were both 5 years old, wearing pretty frocks and holding on to their dolls in Central Park. Their respective governesses brought them to the park daily to play during the warm summer months. Thereon, they grew up together, holding hands.

When they turned 15, their frocks were replaced by miniskirts and their dolls by long cigarettes. They often slept over at each other's house. When they did, they sneaked out, as per Belinda's plan. Belinda, with her brunette bangs, cat eyes, and deep dimples, was the real wild one. Layla had a fear of being lonely, and she followed her dear friend. "Best friends till the end of time," they often announced as they giggled, holding hands and diving deep into each other's drunken eyes. Belinda's precious company took the vacuum away from Layla's life and made everything feel better. She was lively, amusing, light-hearted and jovial. Her only mantra in life was, "Boys, drugs, and rock and roll."

Under the blanket of wild starry nights, after their parents fell fast asleep, they changed out of their pyjamas and into their shortest shimmery skirts. They sneaked out the door and crashed into the closest nightclub, Jazz, wearing heavy makeup and carrying fake IDs. They drank less alcohol and smoked more joints. Belinda danced and flirted with dashing rock artists through the night; Layla enjoyed watching the crowd and smoking her joint. Before dawn, they sneaked back into the house, slipped into their pyjamas, and glided under the covers, pretending to be fast asleep.

One night Layla's parents were woken up by a symphony of purging sounds coming from Layla's bedroom. A bit startled, they walked over to Layla's room and then to the washroom, following the sounds. There they saw the girls vomiting profusely. The head of long blonde hair was bent over the sink, and the head of long brunette hair was bent over the toilet bowl.

"What's the matter with you girls? Is everything okay?" asked Layla's father, a bit worried.

The girls were taken aback at seeing Layla's parents in the room but were able to answer back, lifting up their spinning heads. "Yes, Father, all is well. It's just the cream of mushroom soup that we ate last night. I think it was stale," muttered Layla with feigned innocence on her pretty face.

The parents looked at them doubtingly. "If you girls don't feel better by morning, we'll see the doctor," said Layla's mother, closing the door behind her as they retired to their room.

The girls chuckled as soon as the parents left. Belinda winked at Layla as she whispered, "Yes, the magic mushrooms indeed! The psilocybin mushroom trip and all that partying did get to us." The two giggled again and then resumed their unfinished tasks of purging.

A couple of years later, when the girls turned seventeen going on eighteen, they graduated from their next-door nightclub Jazz to the Scene, the hottest and the most intriguing New York City nightclub. It was a place for jet-setters, Broadway dancers, and New York's moneyed elite. The club hosted a new rock band every few weeks.

Belinda met her short-time fiancé, Neal Park, a member of the rock band The Wise, on the floor of the Scene. Neal was a cute British rock artist with long hair and tight pants. Theirs was love at first sight, and they were lost in love in each other's arms at the Scene's bizarre network of brick-walled cellar rooms and passageways, modelled after cave-style Parisian discos.

One fine evening, to Belinda's pleasant surprise, while they were dancing cheek to cheek, Neal took a step back, knelt on the floor, and offered her a diamond ring while the crowds watched lovingly. They encircled them while the requested Elvis Presley song played in the background. "Take my hand, take my whole life too. I can't help falling in love with you." With tears of joy rolling down her cheeks, Belinda kissed and hugged him as he lifted her up, and the crowd applauded and cheered in the background. They were so in love.

Six months later, Neal dumped Belinda, accusing her of being a groupie, which he had heard through the grapevine. He called off their brief engagement after stories about Belinda being a super groupie started circulating in their common circles.

"Do you even know what groupie means, Neal, before you accuse me of being one?" asked Belinda, glaring ferociously at Neal.

"A groupie is what *you* are, Belinda. I've had hundreds of them fall all over me, and you were just one of them. Just a reckless fan who is more interested in forming relationships with rock stars rather than their music, and she goes all out seeking intimate contact with any member of the band. I certainly do not want a super groupie for a wife, and that is the end of it," Neal said accusingly, jabbing his finger at Belinda's chest as he spoke.

Belinda denied, cried, persuaded, and begged, but to no avail. She was left heartbroken. Layla lent her a shoulder to cry on. Belinda now hated the New York club scene and all the British rock artists. Layla was getting tired of hanging out in the clubs too. She had simply been following her wild friend hither and thither. It all seemed meaningless, and what was it leading to? Layla wanted to live a meaningful life. She wanted to expand her mind and consciousness. She wanted to go on a spiritual odyssey to some mystical land, to obtain answers to questions that invariably echoed in her heart and mind about the purpose of all life and existence.

Layla and Belinda, in their own unique ways, had had enough! Enough of Night Clubs! Enough of make-up and dressing up! Enough of glitter and glamour! Enough of New York! It was time to leave. Having graduated from a spiffy high school, they had to pick a college now. New York didn't seem very appealing to the two. There was yet another place where everyone else seemed to be going: San Francisco!

Layla approached her father one day as he sat on his massive oak desk in an elegantly furnished office, working and sipping on a snifter of cognac and smoking a thick Cuban cigar. "Father, I want to go to San Francisco for further studies. I would like to study at San Francisco State College," said Layla.

"But why? What's wrong with New York?"

"Nothing, Father. It's just not for me."

"Concentrate on your studies, Layla. I do not know where your mind is."

"I know where it is, father, and it is in the right place."

"Have you decided what subject you would like to pursue?" he asked.

"Music."

"Music? Have you lost your mind, Layla? You are my one and only child. Who is going to look after my empire? Who is going to manage my hotels? I want you to study hotel management here in New York, at Cornell University's School of Hotel Administration."

"No, Father. Belinda and I have decided to study music in San Fran."

"Belinda is a bad influence on your life, Layla. Think from your own mind."

"Father, please do not be stubborn. I am going, with or without your blessings. It would be better if I go with your blessings."

"There is nothing I can do if you have already made up your mind, Layla. I wish I had the power to stop you. But I do not, so do as you please," said Layla's father helplessly, throwing his hands up in the air. He paused. "But remember, if at all you happen to change your mind someday, your parents are here for you. We can get you started afresh anytime you want. Okay, Sweetheart?" He had a helpless look in his eyes as he tenderly cupped Layla's face in his hands and kissed her on the forehead. "Take care, my princess."

"Thank you, Father."

They hugged.

Chapter 5

San Francisco

If you are going to San Francisco,
Be sure to wear some flowers in your hair,
If you are going to San Francisco,
You're gonna meet some gentle people there.

— *Scott McKenzie*

1967

One cool and crisp January evening of 1967, after a long and dreary day at San Francisco State College, Layla and Belinda were strolling down the streets of Haight and Ashbury. The streets were full of colourful youngsters wearing flowers in their long, unkempt hair. They were clad in vibrant attire, fringed blouses, flowery vests and jackets, hip-hugger bell bottoms, and grungy jeans. Peace and love symbols circled their necks as they rambled around the intersection that would later be known as the birthplace of Hippie counter-culture movement. Exotic stores lined the streets, live guitar music warbled from corners, a permanent smell of pot wafted in the cool breeze, incense sticks burnt in the window panes of tiny shops, and peace signs hung almost everywhere in colourful hues.

After a slow cruise along the magical street, Layla and Belinda entered an exotic corner gift shop called Kathmandu. It sold little

Buddha statues in silver and brass, tie-dyed clothing, psychedelic paintings, meditation cushions, and Tibetan singing bowls. "Boy, oh boy! I absolutely love this," murmured Layla in a soft, ecstatic voice as she picked up a singing bowl. "Listen." She gently struck the rim of the bowl with a padded mallet. "This is heaven," she whispered, closing her eyes as she listened to the harmonic overtones.

"Hey! What's this?" exclaimed Belinda as she grabbed a copy of San Francisco's leading newspaper, displayed in one corner of the store. Belinda's high-pitched voice disturbed Layla out of her satori. "It says, 'A gathering of the tribes for a Human Be-In on January 14, 1967.'" Belinda's cat eyes were wide open. She brimmed with excitement as she quickly browsed through the post. "Holy cow! This is going to be great. They are protesting against the California law that banned the use of LSD last year. Lots of big shots are going to be there at the event, and they are going to put a lot of sense into people's heads, I believe." She struck a cocky pose and sounded enthralled as she shook her brunette bangs out of her eyes.

Layla simply smiled, still spaced out and relaxed in her bubble of serenity.

"I can't wait to attend this!" exclaimed Belinda, jumping out of her skin.

"Neither can I," said Layla in a monotone, seeming blissfully content as she blankly gazed at the blue sky with dreamy eyes and a peaceful smile.

On the day of the event, Layla, Belinda, and their friends pushed and shoved their way to the front. There was a gathering of some 25,000 people who had showed up at the Golden Gate Park to participate in the Human Be-In. Layla, Belinda, and their flowered friends wanted to be up close to see and hear the famous professor, Dr. Timothy Leary, an ex-Harvard academic who made his first San Francisco appearance that day. He wore flowers on his ears and beads around his neck. He cast a spell on the crowds that afternoon with his famous speech and phrase: "Turn on, tune in, drop out." Dr. Leary spoke about the importance of bringing higher consciousness into the world. He talked about the world and humanity. He described nature, Indian symbols, the meaning of inner life, the LSD experience, and spiritual awakening.

Layla, Belinda, and the crowd stood there, thunderstruck. The counter-culture that evolved at the Human Be-In encouraged the masses to question authority in relation to civil rights and consumer rights, focusing on the key ideas of personal empowerment, communal living, cultural and political decentralization, ecological awareness, acceptance of illicit drug use, and most important, higher consciousness with or without the aid of psychedelic drugs.

Famous speakers, including world-renowned doctors and professors, took the audience by storm through their liberating speeches. Poets chanted mantras as famous rock artists played entrancing music. Layla, Belinda, and the crowd applauded, whistled, cheered, and danced as if possessed by an unknown force—the force of the times.

From that afternoon onwards, Layla became Dr. Leary's ardent fan, quoting his famous phrase from time to time, to friends and foes alike: "Turn on, tune in, drop out." And drop out she did! Spellbound by the spirit of the times, Layla, Belinda, and their friends decided to take a leap of faith. They dropped out of the society and San Francisco State College in the blink of an eye. After that, they formed their own music band, the Purple Smoke, and began living communally in one of the old Victorian homes at the Haight. The Human Be-In had set the stage for San Francisco's Summer of Love.

It was May 1967. Layla, Belinda, and two other members of their band sang Scott McKenzie's "San Francisco" at the Red Victorian Café, their corner hangout joint at Haight. The song had been released that very month and had become an instant hit. It was inspiring thousands of people from world over to travel to San Francisco, "the promised land" to the ones wishing to escape the mainstream, to the one's protesting against the Vietnam War and the materialism of mainstream American society. Like moths to the flame, they came in swarms. As many as 100,000 people converged on the streets of Haight Ashbury. A social phenomenon had occurred. Although hippies also grouped together in other metropolitan cities of Europe, Canada, and the United States, San Francisco remained the epicentre of the social earthquake that would come to be known as the Hippie Revolution. The Golden Gate city was becoming a melting pot of psychedelic music, drugs, and a total lack of social and sexual inhibitions. Alternate lifestyles of communal living and free love were becoming more accepted.

These love rebels often wore flowers in their hair and distributed flowers to passersby, earning them the nickname of flower children. That was what Layla and Belinda called themselves, dancing down the streets of Haight Ashbury amongst people adorned in beads, feathers, flowers, and bells. They had flowers in their hair and garlands around their necks, and they played flutes and guitars. They were full of passion and rebellion.

After they were done playing music and singing in the Red Victorian Café, Layla, Belinda, and their group smoked a joint and mingled in the crowds dancing on the street outside. Layla was scantily clad in a colourful bikini top and a tie-dyed skirt hugging her tiny waist, curvy hips, and shapely long legs. With a garland around her neck that flowed down her full bosom and a bandana of flowers around her forehead, she moved and swayed like a leaf in the gentle breeze to the rhythm of San Francisco.

Layla's parents in New York were particularly upset with her when she informed them about her dropping out of San Fran State College. Unable to make peace with her decision, they made many unsuccessful attempts to convince her of the dangers of her outrageous decision. They tried very hard, over the phone and through letters. But Layla was adamant and stubborn, and she did not budge. She stayed embalmed in her decision. Finally, her parents decided to visit her in July of that year, when summer of love was still in full swing and the love rebels were still hung over after the all-consuming spell that the Monterey Pop Festival had cast on them. This would be her parents' last attempt to dissuade her from living this hedonistic lifestyle and bring her back to New York to live under their protection and care. They wanted for her a sheltered life in an organized college, away from the influence of her hippie friends. But all their effort was in vain. Layla had already made her irrevocable life decision.

After arriving in San Francisco, Layla's mother, Doreen, phoned her from their room at the Ritz Carlton, informing her of their arrival. It did not seem to please Layla very much. "Layla, sweetheart, we are here to see you. Would you like to come to our hotel, or should we drop by at your house?" asked Layla's mother in an almost pleading voice.

"I will come, Mother. It's better that you folks don't bother coming here," answered Layla in a groggy, slurry voice.

Her parents waited an hour, then two, then three. When she did not answer the phone or phone back, they finally called a cab and decided to drive up to her home. The cab parked outside an old, weary Victorian building that wore a washed-out look. Layla's father, David, was finely attired in a tailored Italian suit, with a wide silk tie and a thick Cuban cigar in his mouth. Doreen looked stylish yet sad in her pillbox hat, stiletto shoes, and fitted dress with oversized buttons, reflecting the crème de la crème of the '60s. What went wrong with their daughter, they couldn't understand.

With grief-stricken faces, as if already sensing the impending doom, they cautiously doddered towards the eerie Victorian building, engulfed in feelings of apprehension and fear. Doreen quickly covered her nose with her finely embroidered handkerchief as she smelt marijuana ten feet from the main door. David didn't like hearing the loud psychedelic music that blared from the walls. As they knocked on the main door, a shirtless young man covered in ink and wearing only grungy jeans stuck out his tousled head through the doorway and allowed them in. Young boys and girls wearing colourful clothing—or barely any clothing—sat in a circle on the shaggy carpet, sharing pot. Layla lay her head down on the couch beside them, wearing a bikini top and a batik sarong tied around her waist, confirming her parents' suspicion that she had already had her fill. The edges of her long hair rested mournfully on the floor. The shirtless man tried to wake her up, but she didn't move. After he shook her and jostled her hard for almost 10 minutes, she finally opened her bloodshot eyes, caused by a heavy dose of marijuana. Spaced out as she already was, without having any sense of acknowledging the presence of her parents, she walked straight towards the washroom and then changed into a long, colourful maxi to avoid causing embarrassment to her parents talking or walking with her.

"Let's walk towards the café around the corner for a talk," Layla suggested. Leading her parents out, she walked towards the Red Victorian Café. Frigidly seated inside the café, Doreen nervously sipped her coffee. The trio talked, argued, and yelled. Layla was higher than a Georgia pine, and her parents' words fell on deaf ears.

When finally the two parties reached no conclusion, Layla frustratingly took out a copy of *Time* magazine's current issue, showing them the cover story, entitled "The Hippies: The Philosophy of a Subculture." High on marijuana, she passionately read out loud the article, summarizing the guidelines of the hippie code. She authoritatively moved her head around in gesticulation as she spoke, like a queen stating the hippy commandments. "Do your own thing, wherever you have to do it and whenever you want. Drop out and leave the society as you have known it. Leave it utterly. Blow the mind of every straight person you can reach. Turn them on—if not to drugs, then to beauty, love, honesty, and fun."

After she finished announcing the guidelines of the hippy code, she sighed briefly and then looked her parents in the eye. "Look, Mother and Father. I'm doing the right thing. I'm moving with the times, and I'm doing what everybody else is doing. Doctors, lawyers, and professors—everybody is under the spell of the times. We are working together to create a free, loving, nurturing, and peaceful world. Read this cover story, and listen to Dr. Leary. Try to see what's going on in the world, and please leave me alone to my life. I have no desire to go back to college or to New York. I want to live in a communal setting, playing music with my band. I want to sing, dance, travel, and live a life of love and freedom. Let me be, please."

With these final words she closed the topic, kissed her parents goodbye, and walked into the dark unknown. Her parents had no choice but to let her go.

Chapter 6

Light My Fire

You know that it would be untrue,
You know that I would be a liar,
If I was to say to you,
Girl, we couldn't get much higher.
Come on, baby, light my fire

—Jim Morrison

All good things come to an end, and so did the Summer of Love. Now it was time to light the fire. Overcrowding, homelessness, hunger, drug problems, and crime afflicted the Haight Ashbury district, and as a result, during the fall many students left disheartedly, deciding to resume their college studies. Those who stayed back in Haight, wanted to signal a formal ending to the season of love. A mock funeral, entitled the Death of the Hippie, was staged on October 6, 1967. The intended message was explained by the organizer. "We wanted to signal that this was the end of it, to stay where you are, bring the revolution to where you live, and don't come here. Because it's over and done with." But Layla didn't leave; she was not done yet. A lot was yet to come to shake the ground beneath her feet, now firmly planted in the San Francisco soil.

Layla was disillusioned and heart-broken. Their music band had disintegrated, and people went their separate ways. Their communal home was broken apart. Seeing no other option, Layla requested her parents buy her a separate home. She promised them that she would be rejoining college, and her parents happily did so.

Layla now lived with Belinda in the newly-bought home. Together they laughed, sang, smoked joints, and cracked jokes. Nothing was that bad in Belinda's company. Her roaring laughter made her dimples sink deeper, and the twinkle in her cat eyes cheered up Layla.

One cool yet sunny afternoon in February 1968, Belinda and Layla lay on reclining chairs on the patio of Layla's Victorian home, smoking grass and soaking in sunlight. Belinda was lost in thought, but suddenly she crouched over and pulled out an envelope from her hemp bag. Inside the envelope was a postcard from India. On the front of the postcard was the picture of the Taj Mahal, and on the back were a few lines of text.

> Dear Belinda,
>
> I'm thrilled to announce that I have found my paradise! I am in Goa. I love it here so much that I have decided to make Goa my home forever. I can't explain to you my joy in being here. You belong here! We belong here! The flower children belong here! Leave everything today and come to Goa. Your home, your paradise, your Goa is waiting for you!
>
> Love and peace,
>
> Emily

After reading these lines out loud, Belinda looked towards Layla with hopeful eyes. Layla's eyes shimmered with a newfound dream and excitement, but still somewhere behind that hope lurked suspicion. *What if?* Layla still wanted to give San Francisco a chance;

she wasn't done yet. Soon her glittering eyes gave way to a dull daze at the empty sky. Belinda quietly slipped the postcard back in her bag, realizing that Goa had to wait a little bit longer. Then she gently shook Layla out of here daze.

"Come on, girl. Let's get packed! We are off to Chicago tomorrow" announced Belinda excitedly.

"Chicago? Why?" asked Layla, waking out of her dreams and suspicions.

"It is Pamela's birthday, and she has invited us. Remember Pamela, my groupie friend?" Belinda said while shaking her bangs.

"Yes, yes, of course I remember her!"

"Let's fly away for the weekend. Things have been pretty heavy here in San Fran lately. Let's get a little break."

"Okey-dokey!" said Layla with a smile.

Chicago, February 1968

"Goin' a go-go ... Goin' a go-go ..." Belinda and Layla sang along to the song that played inside Whisky a Go-Go, the first real American discotheque, on the corner of Rush Street and Chestnut Street. It opened in 1958 in Chicago, and it owed its name to the first discotheque ever, which was opened in Paris by Paul Pacine. Whisky a Go-Go was one of the places that popularized go-go dancing in America. Belinda and Layla were to meet Pamela over here.

The club rocked as Pamela entered with her group of friends. She wore a tiny shimmery black dress beneath her ankle-length fur coat. She flung her coat on the sofa as she saw Belinda and Layla seated at the corner table by the elevated dance floor, on which sexy blondes danced inside a poled cage. Dressed in sparkling red shorts and glittering red bras, their big, beehived hair swirled all over their faces as they jerked and shook their heads in sheer ecstasy to the music played by the sleek, mop-top rock artists of the live band, who were dressed in pencil pants, ties, and blazers while jamming on their guitars and driving the girls crazy.

"Woo-hoo! Hey, girlies! There you are!" greeted Pamela. She was a tall, nifty, strawberry-blonde with green eyes and waist-length hair that covered most of her alluring face. Her pouted lips and manicured long nails were painted bright red. The girls hugged each other, jumping out of their skins with wide grins and dilated pupils.

Cake cutting and happy birthday singing was followed by laughing, floor tapping, dancing, giggling, drinking, and sniffing. It continued all night, with frequent trips to the ladies room for powder pleasure.

"I love that Jim Morrison tattoo you have on your arm, girl," shouted Pamela from across the table, over the sound of blaring rock music.

"Thanks. I love the guy! He's my god!" Layla shouted back with a wink.

"What? Your god? Ha!" Pamela laughed, tilting her head back as she continued. "I love the guy too, and I've got a story to tell you. Tomorrow morning. Remind me, okay?" She winked as she pointed her index finger at Layla mischievously.

"Okey-dokey," said Layla as the girls resumed their dancing.

The sun welcomed the girls with pounding headaches. Morning coffee at Mama's, the corner café, was decided upon as the cure instead of another line of coke—a traditional, tried-and-tested remedy popular with Belinda.

"Hey, Pamela. You were saying something about my tattoo last night?" prompted Layla with a curious frown as Layla and Pamela sat at a corner table for two, sipping coffee.

"Oh, yeah! I tell ya, the god of rock is the most beautiful man on the face of this earth. I've got a story. Wanna hear?" teased Pamela.

"I'm dying to. Please tell me," urged Layla, leaning forward with her hands cupped around the warm cup of coffee.

"Okay, then listen. One fine evening in Hollywood hills, while high on PCP, I ended up in the rock god's house in Laurel Canyon. Can you believe that?" said Pamela with her green eyes wide open as she pounded on the wooden table, almost knocking over her cup of coffee. Layla leaned over the table and held her breath as Pamela continued. "As I walked lost in ecstasy, I heard 'The End' playing from a house nearby, and I wandered off into it. There he was, standing next to his refrigerator, bare-chested in unzipped leather pants, singing along with his own record. The rock god incarnate! In no time we were making out passionately on his Persian rug. It was that simple, that easy."

"Whoa! You lucky girl!" exclaimed Layla in astonishment.

"Yes, indeed! Lucky I am," said Pamela with a wink and a smile as she leaned back, clasping her fingers behind her head.

A few days full of dance and laughter were good enough to distract Layla from what was going on in San Francisco, at least temporarily. Come Sunday night, they were back in the Golden Gate city. Things were not the same as before. Barely six months had passed after the mock funeral of the hippie, and the world was suddenly hit with the news of the assassination of the leader of the African American civil rights movement, Martin Luther King Jr. on April 4, 1968. People had hardly recovered from the shock of his death when, two months later on June 6, Robert F. Kennedy was gunned down in the pantry of the Ambassador Hotel in Los Angeles. The age of free love was dying down and barely breathing, and the dark demon of death seemed to be towering over it, stifling it. Things seemed dismal and grey as Layla and Belinda plodded down a quiet street of Haight in June of 1968.

An image of a short-statured man with shoulder-length hair seemed to be emerging out of the darkness, blocking out any remaining light of the setting sun. The man was dressed in a maroon velvet shirt and maroon corduroy bellbottoms, and he seemed to be waving at them.

"Layla! Hey, Layla! It's me!" The figure waved as it briskly approached the girls.

"Charlie? What are you doing here?" mumbled Layla, seeming a little surprised by the man's sudden appearance.

"I am visiting San Fran for a day. I now live with my family on the outskirts of Los Angeles. What are you doing these days?" asked the man.

"Umm ... I'm on a spiritual quest," said Layla after a moment of reflection. "I'm searching for something. I don't know what, though. Something that can give some deep meaning to my life," stated Layla contemplatively. "What about you?"

"I am trying to save the chosen few," said the man, crossing his arms across his chest and tapping his foot as he continued passionately. "You see the killings and shootings, and the assassination of Martin Luther King Jr. Where do you think we are heading?" He placed his hands on his hips. When Layla did not answer, he continued with the answer to his own question. "Of course, towards an impending apocalyptic race war, because of all this racial tension between blacks and whites. Come for my talk one day. I would like to include you in my chosen few. Give me your phone number, please." The man spoke intensely, as if granting Layla a huge boon.

Layla seemed a bit intimidated by him. She hurriedly scribbled down her phone number for him on a piece of paper and then waved goodbye. The last thing Layla needed right now was more terror stories.

After the man walked away, Belinda turned towards Layla. She shook her brunette bangs and pointed her index finger towards Layla as she forcefully instructed, "Don't even think about it, Layla. There is something macabre about this man. Forget that you ever met him."

Layla sighed "Boy, oh boy!" She nodded in consent as the two girls walked away into the darkness.

Layla had known Charlie from San Francisco's summer of love. She had met him a number of times at a mutual friend's house, where Charlie often came to obtain some marijuana. Apart from being a musician, singer, and songwriter, he was also a former convict who had spent half of his adolescent years in correctional institutions, and he was involved in various offences. Nevertheless, a pop culture had arisen around him, and he had established himself as a guru in Haight Ashbury during the Summer of Love. Some said he borrowed philosophically from the process church, whose members worshipped Satan. The last Layla had seen him was in November 1967, when he left San Francisco with maybe ten of his followers in an old-school bus. Layla had had a chance meeting with him at one of the intersections, while he was leaving. Layla had taken a quick peek inside the bus as the two waved goodbye, and she still remembered how groovy the bus looked. It had been decorated in hippy style, with colourful rugs and pillows in place of the removed seats. The group had plans of travelling all over the United States, Charlie had informed her before parting. Now it seemed they had settled somewhere around LA.

Layla didn't think much of this meeting because she didn't have any plans of seeing him again.

The next morning, Layla sat in a lotus position on the porch of her house with her closed eyes, trying to meditate upon her life. Next to her lay Belinda, propped on an elbow and puffing out billows of marijuana smoke. "Belinda, I want to meditate," stated Layla calmly with closed eyes. "Maybe ... um, I want to follow Maharishi Mahesh Yogi and learn some transcendental meditation." She opened her eyes as she looked towards Belinda inquisitively.

"Oh, yeah! I heard that the Beatles just got back after spending some time at his ashram in Rishikesh, India. But they weren't particularly satisfied, you know," stated Belinda nonchalantly as she puffed out a cloud of smoke and watched two birds flying a loop the loop in the blue sky.

"I know of some tensions between them. Some say that there was some financial disagreement. There were also rumours of inappropriate behaviour by the guru. People on Maharishi's side say that the Beatles and their entourage were doing drugs and taking LSD at Maharishi's ashram. The Maharishi was completely intolerant of it, and so they broke apart. Who knows the truth, and who cares!" said Layla, shrugging her shoulders and pulling down the corners of her lips.

"Yeah, who knows, and who cares!" Belinda turned to look at Layla. "There is nothing wrong with you desiring to meditate. Why don't we go to India and find our kind of guru? Someone a bit wild, a cool and freaky kind of guru." Belinda gave a dimpled grin and had a mischievous look in her eyes.

"A freaky guru? Ha!" Layla broke out into an uncontrollable fit of laughter. "And where do you think we'll find him?"

"We will! In the freak land of Goa. My heart says so. You know that Goa's calling, right, Layla?"

"I know, Belinda. And I know that we will eventually go to Goa. I also know that once I go, I am never coming back. But that will happen only when the time is ripe. For now, "West is the Best, the West is the Best."

Belinda continued singing from where Layla ended as she walked inside the house. "The blue bus is calling us ..."

Belinda walked back out with two blue pills of the hallucinogenic cactus, peyote, referred to as the blue deer by the Huicholes, a tribe in the northern Mexican desert.

Something else was brewing in the deserts. Haight Ashbury's Charlie was making preparation for his predicted racial war. Two major influences on the mind of Charlie, which led him to orchestrate the ghastly murders, were the Beatles and the Book of Revelations. He often quoted the Beatles and the Bible to his "family members" who had joined him over time, starting mainly from his influence in the hippy locale of San Francisco and his US tour, covering as far north as Washington state and then heading southward through Los Angeles and Mexico. Finally he returned to and settled down in the Los Angeles area. In Charlie's distorted mind, the Book of Revelation and the Beatles were strongly linked. He saw the four members of the music band as the four angels referred to in Revelation 9. Revelation 9 also tells of locusts—the Beatles, in Charlie's mind, "coming out upon the earth." It describes prophets as having "faces as faces of the men," but "with the hair of women," an assumed reference to the long hair of all male English groups. The four angels "with breast plates of fire" (electric guitars) issued "fire and brimstone" (song lyrics). Charlie believed that the artists of the Beatles group spoke to him through their lyrics, especially those included in the White Album, released in November 1968.

Most of the songs of the White Album were written during the group's stay at Maharishi's ashram in India during their transcendental meditation course. Several songs from the album confirmed Charlie's belief in the forthcoming revolt by blacks against white supremacy. When the album came out, Charlie listened to it over and over again. He thought that the Beatles were talking about what he had been expounding for years. He interpreted many of the songs idiosyncratically, thus reinforcing his belief that the group was communicating directly with him through their songs.

The phone rang in Layla's San Francisco house. She picked it up and said, "Hello?"

"Hi, it's Charlie. How have you been?"

"I am fine. And you?"

"You can't be fine, Layla. I want to save you from the impending disaster. Come join my family. At least come and hear what I have to say. Join me for New Year's Eve, and I will reveal everything. Take down my address"

Layla wrote down the address and hastily said goodbye. The phone call disturbed Layla, but in order to give the man a fair chance, Layla decided to go for the talk, against Belinda's warnings. They met halfway, agreeing that after Layla visited the group, Belinda would stay in hiding nearby in their car and would wait for at least an hour. If Layla smelt foul play, she would quietly sneak back into the car, and the two would drive away.

On a cold New Year's Eve, Layla and Belinda arrived at Myer's Ranch, near California's Death Valley. Belinda stayed in hiding while Layla stepped forward and was greeted by Charlie's family. They gathered around a large fire and listened as Charlie talked. Layla sat behind everyone in a shady nook.

"The social turmoil that I have been predicting for long has been predicted by the Beatles in their White Album. The songs are telling it all, although in codes. In fact, the entire album is directed at us, our family, and we are being encouraged by the group to preserve the worthy from the impending disaster. We have to prepare for Helter Skelter. Are you hep to what the Beatles are saying? Helter Skelter is coming down. The group is telling it like it is. The blacks are gonna go up, and the whites are gonna go down. We will now create an album with songs whose messages are going to be as subtle as those of the Beatles. This will trigger the conflict by encouraging America's white youth to join our esteemed family. Young female white hippies will be drawn out of San Francisco's Haight Ashbury due to the power of our songs. Black men, thus deprived of white women, will be without an outlet for their frustration and will then indulge in violent crimes against the whites. A resultant murderous rampage against blacks by frightened whites will then be exploited by militant blacks to provoke a war between racist and non-racist whites over the treatment of the black man, thus turning the cities into an inferno of racial revenge. Then the militant blacks will arise to completely finish off the few surviving whites.

"In this holocaust the members of our enlarged family will have little to fear. We will wait for the war to finish in a secret city that lies underneath the Death Valley, which we will reach through a hole in the ground. We will then be the only remaining whites and will emerge from the underground to rule the now satisfied blacks, who will be unable of running the world because of their innate incapability. I would scratch the black man's fuzzy head, kick him in the butt, and tell him to go pick the cotton and be a good nigger. It will be our world, then. There will be no one except us and the black servants. I, Charlie, the fifth angel, Jesus Christ, will rule the world along with other four angels, the Beatles." The family around the fire applauded and started singing like insane fanatics.

Charlie continued his talk as Layla sat in the back with a racing pulse, a pounding heart, and a parched throat. Signalling to a neighbour that she was going to use the washroom, she tiptoed towards Belinda in hiding. After several minutes, when she knew that her footsteps would not be heard, she ran as fast as she could towards the car. Seeing Layla run from a distance, Belinda flung opened the door and started the engine as Layla jumped inside, and the two drove off at lightning speed.

Layla mumbled in shock and fear with her head resting on the window and her eyes half shut. "There is going to be bloodshed and war. The madman is going to kill people. He will kill me because I know everything. We have to run away. We have to run away now if we want to survive. Take me across the seas, Belinda. The time has come."

The two went back to their San Francisco house to pick up their passports and clothes. They stayed the night at a hotel, fearing that Charlie would come looking for her at her house. The next morning, they drove to LA and checked into a hotel before flying to Europe. Layla called her parents in New York to inform them of her plans of travelling to Europe.

"Mother, I'll send you the keys to our San Fran house. Keep them safe; I might need them one day."

"I don't understand, Darling. Why do you have to leave? What's the emergency?"

"I can't explain much at the moment, other than that I have to leave."

"Okay, Love. Try to stay safe. Do you have enough money in the bank to support you in your venture?"

"Yes! For the moment, it seems I have enough! But if I fall short, I won't hesitate to ask."

"Sounds good, Honey! Please keep writing to us. Your father certainly won't be very pleased to hear about you leaving, but we have no hope left," her mom said with bitter sarcasm coming out of her aching heart.

"Take care, Mother. Love you. Bye."

"Bye, Love," said a disappointed mother.

Belinda suggested that they fly to Luxembourg and spend a few months travelling around Europe. Then from somewhere in Europe, they could board a cheap, private bus to India, following the hippie trail that all the hippies were taking. Layla agreed, and the two booked their flight to Luxembourg. The date of the flight was two days later. Belinda and Layla prepared for their trip.

One night before leaving, Belinda and Layla visited Barney's Beanery, close to the Sunset Strip, for a couple of drinks. As they walked out of the bar, they saw a man lying by the roadside with his head down in the gutter. His shoulder-length hair covered most of his face as he mumbled something. Layla quickly walked up to him and turned him around. It was no other than her god in her lap. The god of rock, drunk and stoned, bearded and fat, looked at her with partly closed eyes. Her god was going down with time; excessive drinking and drug use had taken a toll on the star. This formerly svelte singer's signature leather pants and concho belts had been replaced by casual jeans and T-shirts over his fat belly.

"Thank you, girl," mumbled the star in a slurred voice "Can you help me walk inside? I want to treat you to a drink."

Suddenly a man came rushing towards him. "Hey, Buddy, what happened? I was looking for you everywhere. How did you get here in this state?"

The star could hardly answer his question and looked at Layla. "Come inside, girl."

"No, thank you. I have to go. You take care of your precious self," said Layla, choked up and trying to keep her composure as tears welled up in her blue eyes. She turned her back upon her god as she unleashed her tears. As the two friends walked away, Layla stared into emptiness and narrated a parable of a famous Indian poet, Rabindra Nath Tagore.

"I have been seeking and searching for God for as long as I can remember. And to my surprise, one day I reached a house in a far-away star with a small sign in front of it saying, 'This is the house of God.' My joy knew no bounds—so finally I have arrived! I rushed up the steps, many steps that lead to the door of the house. But as I was coming closer and closer to the door, a fear suddenly gripped my heart. As I was going to knock, I became paralyzed with a fear that I had never known, never thought of, never dreamt of. The fear was, if this house is certainly the house of God, then what will I do after I have found him? Now that searching for God has become my very life, and to have found him will be equivalent to committing suicide. And what am I going to do with him? I had never thought of all these things before. I should have thought before I started the search: What am I going to do with God?

"I took my shoes in my hands, and silently and very slowly stepped back, afraid that God may hear the noise and may open the door and say, 'Where are you going? I am here, come in!' And as I reached the steps, I ran away as I have never run before. Since then I have been again searching for God, looking for him in every direction—and avoiding the house where he really lives. Now I know that house has to be avoided. I continue the search and enjoy the very journey, the pilgrimage."

Layla stopped walking and slowly turned around to look at Belinda. Belinda opened her arms, and Layla broke into hysterical tears, hugging her tightly while Belinda gently caressed her back.

The next morning, Layla and Belinda boarded the Icelandic Airlines to Luxembourg. They spent five years instead of six months travelling around Europe and the Middle East. Belinda modelled to support her travels, and Layla had her parents' money on which to rely. They sent her a monthly allowance in her bank each month. Layla loved her parents for their generosity.

While Layla and Belinda travelled across Europe, the world was once again shaken up by the news of brutal murders of an American actress Sharon Tate and a well-known supermarket executive Leno La Bianca and his wife on August 9–10, 1969. Though Layla felt deep pain for those who were murdered, in the same breath, she couldn't thank her stars enough for how she had narrowly escaped getting embroiled in a criminal web of insanity. After all, she knew who the orchestrator of the murders was, even though the world yet didn't know. She knew what "Death to Pigs," "Rise," and "Helter Skelter" meant; the phrase were found written in blood on the walls of the victims' house. Layla wanted to stay as far away from this chaos as she possibly could. She heaved a sigh of relief and moved on.

For their travels around Europe, Layla and Belinda bought a car from Paris and painted it in vibrant colours with a purple base. There was a pink peace sign on the hood and bright yellow sunflowers on the roof of the Volkswagen Beetle. The two were still travelling around Paris in their funky car when the news of the death of the god of rock, Jim Morrison shocked the world on July 3, 1971. The earth shook beneath Layla's feet when she heard that her god was found dead in the bathtub of his Paris apartment. Layla was devastated by the news at first, but she finally felt better after she concluded, as most of the star's fans did, that Jim had probably faked his death in order to live an obscure yet peaceful life somewhere in the jungles of Africa, to write poetry. Her world was beautiful again, and her god was immortal.

With love in their hearts, hope in their eyes, and dance in their step, Layla and Belinda boarded an overland bus travelling from Athens to India in August 1974.

Chapter 7

India, India

India, India! Take me to your heart,
Reveal all your ancient mysteries to me,
I'm searching for some answers.

—*John Lennon*

1974

Layla and Belinda sat huddled in the colourful magic bus, which was crammed with young dreamers and nosing its way into India. Painted in stimulating and vibrant psychedelic art, the bus was zipping its way across the borders of Greece, Turkey, Iran, Afghanistan, Pakistan, and then India, the never-never land. Layla craned her neck, sticking it out of the colourful window to let the warm wind blow against her dust-covered face. Her uncombed, unkempt, and unshampooed blonde hair flew in disarray about her face as she sang along with the blasting rock music that played in the bus. "The bus came by, and I got on, that's when it all began, there was cowboy Neal, at the wheel of a bus to never-ever land ..."

They had been on the road for six weeks before they made their first stop in Delhi. John and Janice, along with a few others who were on their way to Kathmandu, were getting off here. The two were old-time hippies who had already spent a few years travelling around India and Nepal; they were returning back to Kathmandu after spending a few months in Europe. Layla, Belinda, John, and Janice had formed a great friendship in these six weeks on road. John and Janice had educated and informed them of dos and don'ts in India. How to deal with beggars, how to look through scam artists, how to bargain, where to live in Goa—they had imparted this important knowledge to them.

"Hopefully we will meet again, girls. It was great knowing you both! Enjoy the adventure!" said John with a wink and thumbs-up.

"Have fun, girlies!" said Janice as she hugged and kissed goodbye with her dry, cracked lips.

"Bye, Janice and John," said Layla and Belinda.

Their next stop was in Bombay. A handsome young man with shoulder-length, silky blond hair and a well-sculpted face and body boarded the bus. Dressed in white harem pants and a white vest, the man smiled at Layla and Belinda as he passed by them and sat on the vacant seat behind the two. The handsome man seemed friendly and attractive. "Hi, girls. I'm André," he greeted in a tuneful French accent.

Layla and Belinda had turned around to scan the newly boarded passenger crowd behind them. "Hi, André!" greeted the girls with wide smiles, and they noticed the intricately designed tattoo of Lord Shiva on his arm.

"That's a groovy tattoo," commented Belinda.

"Hey, thanks!" said André with a smile. The silver *Shiva lingam* (silver phallus) hanging around André's neck shimmered in Belinda's eye as he said, "Where are you girls heading to?"

"To Goa," muttered Layla hastily, waving at a fly that buzzed in her ear.

"The flies are really bothering you, aren't they?" He chuckled as his tanned and tattooed hand waved another fly off Layla.

"Boy, oh boy! Yes, they are. I can't wait to take a shower and get all this caked dirt off my sticky body," wailed Layla as sweat poured down her face.

"Well, I have an idea, *mes chéries*! While we are parked, I can walk you girls to my friend's house around the corner, where I was staying. You can take a shower, if you like. We are parked here for an hour at least," offered André.

"Hey, that'll be great! We can also stretch our legs and enjoy the rest of the ride into India," said Layla, jumping at the offer. "Come on, Belinda. Let's go!" She pulled Belinda by the arm.

André, Layla, and Belinda walked in scorching heat of the afternoon sun while cars, auto rickshaws, and scooters on the road blasted their horns. They walked with beads of sweat shining on their foreheads and noses till they reached the end of the block, and then they walked up a fleet of stairs and headed into a tiny apartment. An Indian man sat on brown velvet covered sofa reading *Times of India* while his wife, wearing a sari with a long swinging braid down to her hips, was handing him a tiny white cup of tea with a cookie in the saucer.

"Hey, friend! You are back?" inquired the Indian man with a look of surprise. His short black hair was neatly trimmed, oiled, and parted to the side. His pencil thin moustache reminded Layla of the heroes of the 1930s black-and-white films that she used to watch as a little girl.

"These girls I befriended on the bus need to use the washroom, if you don't mind," André said politely.

"Of course, go ahead," said the Indian with a cheerful smile.

His wife handed the girls a pink pack of Lux soap. Layla went in first while two little girls, the couple's daughters, stood outside the washroom door right next to Belinda, whispering and giggling while keeping their eyes affixed on her. Belinda smiled at them while they ogled at her.

"Ah, I feel so fresh!" exclaimed Layla as she walked out of the washroom after washing off layers of dirt accumulated from over five countries. It was Belinda's turn now. Once done, the wife offered the girls and André chilled glasses of a red drink. "Have a Roohafza, please" the Indian man said "It's a very refreshing drink ideal for hot summer months. My wife made it in filtered water."

"Thank you," replied Layla, Belinda, and André as they hurriedly guzzled down the sweet red drink.

"Thank you for letting us take a shower," said Layla and Belinda.

"You are very welcome," said the Indian man with an extremely wide grin as he bowed his head, seeming pleased.

"Thank you, friend," said André, flicking his hair to a side, away from his blue eyes as he gave the Indian man a hug.

The two little girls walked behind Layla, Belinda, and André till the end of the stairway, giggling all the way. "Bye! Bye!" they shouted as the trio walked out of sight.

"Paisa, madam hungry," Layla heard someone say as a hand tugged on her dress. She turned around to see a little boy dressed in a long, soiled shirt hanging down to his knees with an extended palm.

"Hungry, madam. Please, money," said a little girl to Belinda, motioning towards her mouth.

"I don't have Indian currency on me," said Layla to André with a look of guilt on her face.

André gave the little boy and the little girl a coin each.

Three more kids came running towards them. "Paisa, sir, hungry," cried one. "Paisa, madam, no food," wailed another.

"Okay, girls, I have no more change left on me. Walk fast if you don't want to get mauled," said André with a grin as he flicked his hair to the side and shooed away the children. "No change, finish. Please go."

They walked briskly towards the bus with a horde of barefoot children in tattered clothes scurrying behind them, tugging on to their shirts. "Paisa, please." "Money, please. Hungry."

Layla jump-stepped on the bus, heaving a sigh of relief. "Boy, oh boy! I was not ready for that. I feel so sorry for these little children. I wish I had Indian money on me," she lamented, looking mournfully in the direction of the children.

"Don't you worry, *ma chérie*. You will get ample opportunity to donate while travelling around India," said André with a smile as they seated themselves. The driver started the engine, and the bus was on its way, covering the final lap of the journey from Bombay to Goa and then to Calangute, a small town in North Goa—their destination. Layla and Belinda spent the rest of the 24 hours listening to tales of Goa as narrated by André. André was an old-timer and an insider who had already spent a couple of years living in Goa. Layla and Belinda were ecstatic to befriend him.

"You girls are going to love Goa!" he said with a preposterous amount of excitement as he flicked his long blond hair to the side. "It stands apart from the rest of India. Goa was a Portuguese colony until 1961, so you will see a lot of cultural influence of the Portuguese here, especially in housing, style, and architecture. Even my house in Goa is built in Portuguese style. You girls are going to love it! Wait and watch." He had a twinkle in his eye.

"You have a house in Goa?" asked Belinda with a look of surprise on her face.

"Yes, I do. Right on the beach!" He beamed and then continued. "There are also many heritage Portuguese houses and churches in Goa. It is a small state with a small population. Unlike Bombay and Delhi, you won't see many beggars or much traffic on the roads." He gave a mischievous smile, nudging Layla, who smiled back. "And of course, you are going to fall in love with our hippie community.

It's heaven on earth—unbelievable, unimaginable." André babbled on while Layla and Belinda listened without batting an eyelid.

Finally the bus crossed the border of Goa, and they were now driving through the Goan countryside. Layla and Belinda were overawed by the lush greenery that surrounded them. Tall coconut, and palm, mango, and cashew trees shrouded the narrow, winding roads through old villages. Layla extended her arm out of the window to touch and feel the fresh greenery. *Thump! Thump!* Coconuts fell on the roof of the bus, prompting Layla to pull her arm back in. "What was that?" she shrieked.

"Coconuts dancing on the roof," André said with a laugh. Then came a vast stretch of rice paddy fields near the narrow country roads. Despite the almost empty road, the bus driver kept slowing down periodically, first to let some cows cross the road, and then to let chickens cross. Finally came the vast turquoise ocean, which was calm and serene. Tall palms bowed down to its majesty, leaning over it. Purple-hued Portuguese houses stood perched on little hillocks on the opposite side.

"We are here! We have arrived in Calangute, dear friends," announced the bus driver as he parked the bus in a small square by the sea.

Passengers clapped and cheered. They collected their baggage, thanked the driver, and dispersed in different directions. Layla, Belinda, and André stepped down from the bus and walked towards its rear to collect their baggage.

"Do you live around here?" inquired Layla, crouching over the trunk to reach for her belongings.

"No. I live on Anjuna beach, a couple of hours from here. That's where the hippie community lives," answered André, extending his tanned and tattooed arm to help Layla and Belinda grab their luggage. "You girls are most welcome to be my guests till you find a place of your own," he offered.

"Holy cow! You are so kind, André!" chirped Belinda as she leaped on him and knocked him off his step, to give him a tight hug.

"Thank you, André," murmured Layla as she hugged him and kissed him on the cheek.

"You are most welcome *mes chéries*," answered André courteously with a twinkle in his eye. "How about a cold glass of mango shake before we start our trek? We have to wade through a river and climb over a hill to reach Anjuna beach."

"Really?" exclaimed Belinda and Layla, gaping at him and stunned by the revelation.

The three of them walked over to a paved square. Tiny palm leaf shacks, called chai shops, lined the paved area. André walked into a little shack called Going Bananas. A rusty metallic board hung on the outside and listed a variety of fresh fruit juice and shakes that they offered in misspelled English. Layla chose Stroberry Shak, and Belinda had an Orange Joos. André waved and smiled at familiar faces passing by as he placed the order. Travellers with sandy bare feet and salted, tanned bodies filled the chai shops.

The three of them sat at a rickety table. André drank coconut water with a straw out of a green coconut. A strand of his hair fell over his forehead, but he didn't flick it to a side this time. *He looks cute,* thought Belinda. His eyes looked hazily towards the ocean, over which the yellow sun was shining bright, causing the ocean to glitter in its sparkling light. Tree leaves rustled in the gentle breeze. A crow cawed in the background.

"*Mes chéries,* we have to hurry up now if we want to reach Anjuna before sunset," said André as he tossed the coconut shell in the garbage can.

"Okey-dokey," said Layla.

"We are all set to go," said Belinda, standing up straight.

It was 5:00 p.m., and soon they were on their way. They walked down the beach, waded through the shallow waters of Baga River, and climbed over a hill following a rocky dirt path. As they descended the hill, André stepped over a boulder and pointed downwards ecstatically. "That's Anjuna." Nothing much could be seen in the fading sunlight except thick covers of the palm treetops that shrouded everything. They sprinted the rest of the way down in excitement.

The girls followed André into a chai shop called High Tea. "Hi, Pinto!" said André to a guy behind the counter.

"Hi, André! You are back! Great to see you, friend," came the Indian-accented reply from a short-haired man wearing a white vest and beige creased shorts. This chai shop seemed a little different from the others in terms of size and customers. It was much bigger, and the customers were hardcore hippies who had made this place their home; they were not plain tourists visiting for a holiday.

A tall woman with long strawberry-blonde hair wore an orange bikini top with a long, flowing skirt in elephant design. She sat amongst a group of foreigners who were passing a chillum of hashish. "Bam Bhole," yelled a man with matted hair before puffing out clouds of grey smoke. The blonde woman tiptoed towards André and then lunged on him from behind. "Hey, André! I missed you! You are back."

"Hey, Laura! I missed you too, *ma chérie!*" replied André with a smile and a hug.

"Are you coming for the sunset?" she inquired.

"Yes, sure, now that we are on time. My friends would love to see it. Meet Layla and Belinda. We met on the bus. Girls, this is American Laura"

After exchanging courteous hellos, Laura left to rejoin the group. A male voice yelled out, "Bam Shankar!" Soon another voice bellowed, "Bam Bhole!" Layla and Belinda looked at each other, perplexed. It did not go unnoticed by André.

"For your information, *mes chéries*, Bam Bhole and Bam Shankar is chanted before smoking a chillum to invoke Lord Shiva's blessings upon the chillum and the smoker. It's like seeking his permission to smoke," he explained with a wide smile. He then added, "Another important thing to know about our community here, which may appear very confusing, is that because we all have dropped our family names and last names, whenever there are two people with duplicate first names, a descriptive adjective or a nickname is given to both. Here we have an English Neal and a German Neal, an American Laura and an Italian Laura, and a Canadian André and a French André—that is me." He flicked his hair to the side.

"Thank you, André—or rather, French André," said Layla with a grin.

"What would we do without you, Sweetheart?" said Belinda.

"And what is this, um, coming for sunset?" asked Layla.

"Ah! That's the communal sunset. It is a ritual. You see, the people who live here, including me, have renounced our families and homelands for good. We don't talk about our birth families or our past. We have come here in search of a utopian land, or rather to create a new utopian land. We want a natural world full of love, freedom, peace, music, and dance. The communal sunset is a ritualistic reminder of why we are here."

"Sounds great!" said Layla, sizzling with excitement and enthusiasm.

"Let's go. I can't wait to see it," said Belinda, rubbing together the palms of her hands.

The three walked towards the beach, which was filling up with people. André waved and smiled at friendly and familiar faces that looked towards him in recognition. Long-haired and scantily-clad young people trickled in from all directions. They browsed around, found their comfortable spots on the sand, and settled in. The men wore a rectangular loincloth wrapped around their hips, called a lungi, and women wore long skirts in bright colours, mostly tie-dyed or an Indian print of flowers, peacocks, and camels. Most women wore a bikini top or were bare-chested with silver jewellery jingling around their arms, necks, and ankles. Many wore flowers in their hair and around their necks.

"Let's sit here," said André after finding a scenic spot. Everyone seemed calm, serene, and still as they looked steadily towards the horizon, where the orange sun was sinking behind the blue ocean, turning the sky shades of scarlet and amethyst. Everything was aglow in the pink-orange hue of the setting sun. It seemed like everyone had gathered here to pray in silence, though there was no church or temple, just nature and its bounty in the fading light of the western sky.

After sunset, everyone dispersed for dinner. They flashed serene smiles and waved their hands at one another as they left. "Let's go and eat at Pete's Restaurant. You girls are going to love the food he offers," suggested André.

"Okey-dokey!" said Layla

"Sure! I am famished. Thank you, dear André," said Belinda "I am also very tired and sleepy. How far is your house from here?"

"Not very far. We have a 10-minute walk to the restaurant, and another 10 minutes to my house."

"Sounds great! Let's go!" shouted Belinda with feigned gusto.

André switched on his pocket flashlight, and the three walked through a corner of a paddy field and through a ravine to reach Pete's Restaurant, which was shrouded by tall palms and tropical flowers. Luminous fireflies buzzed around flashing magical light. Kerosene pump lamps hung from trees; electricity had not yet reached the naturalistic Anjuna beach. A group of people sat huddled together on the porch of the restaurant, passing chillum and periodically chanting "Bam Bhole" or "Bam Shankar."

The three seated themselves around a wooden table with a candle burning in the middle. André browsed over the usual misspelled menu and ordered "chicken soop," "baked fish with vegtables," and "fish cotlets." The three calmly enjoyed their meal in the enchanting, picturesque setting.

"Thank you. This was truly delicious," commented Layla.

"Finger-licking good," agreed Belinda, shaking her brunette bangs and twinkling her cat eyes.

A three-quarter moon hung low over the paddy field as the three walked through it. Palm tree leaves rustled in the light wind. Nothing could be heard but the ocean waves softly crashing against the rocky beach.

"Ta-da! We are home," said André, unlocking the main door of a beautiful house perched on a hillock right by the beach. "Welcome, *mes chéries.*" André stood against the opened door, allowing Layla and Belinda to walk in. André lit the candles and the kerosene lamps that were hung in a decorative manner around the house. The house was decorated with batik wall hangings, Tibetan paintings, satin-covered mattresses and cushions, Afghani rugs, and a huge portrait of Lord Shiva that adorned the central wall. After walking the girls through the house, André finally showed them their room on the top floor. Layla and Belinda thanked André with a hug and a kiss and then crashed on their beds.

Chapter 8

Hello! I Love You

She's walking down the street,
Blind to every eye she meets,
Do you think you'll be the guy,
To make the queen of the angels sigh
— Jim Morrison

Layla woke up to the crowing of the roosters in the morning. There was a dance in her step as she bounced out of her bed and swung open the window that faced the sea. Fresh ocean breeze swept across her face. The large orange ball of fire slowly started rising over the ocean, enveloping everything in its orangeness. The sea was ablaze in its pink and orange hues. Crows cawed lazily perched on the branches of tall trees.

Hearing a knock on the door Layla slid open its wooden bolt. "Hello, girlies. The tea is ready," André said with a smile. Layla woke up Belinda and the three of them sat around a wooden table, sipping masala chai prepared by André's *ayah,* named Rosie. She was a cook, a cleaner, and a caretaker of the house, all in one.

"Thank you for the delicious chai, Rosie," said Belinda.

"Thank you Rosie," said Layla. Rosie smiled back and resumed shelling green peas for lunch.

Layla and Belinda talked about how well they'd slept through the night and how much they were already falling in love with the place. "I don't want to spend the rest of my life anywhere in this world but here, in Goa. Goa is my home, the heaven on earth I had been searching for all this time," Belinda passionately stated. "Yes! Undoubtedly so. I didn't even know that this little world actually existed. We searched everywhere—New York, San Francisco, and all over Europe. Goa is what I have been looking for all my life. My only regret is that I didn't find this place earlier," mumbled Layla, scrunching her face.

"There is timing for everything in life, Layla. You couldn't have come here before the time was ripe for you to be in Goa. You had to go through all your experiences in New York, San Francisco, and Europe in order to be able to appreciate what Goa has to offer. Maybe you wouldn't have liked Goa had you come here five years back," explained André patiently, his words dripping with wisdom.

"Yes, you are so right! Where do you get all your wisdom from?" asked Layla, leaning towards him. Her eyes suddenly fell upon an old, rustic bookrack placed in a corner. "Ah! From these books!" She walked towards the rack full of books on the Vedas, Upanishads, Vedic Astrology, and Kundalini, quickly leafing through one of them.

"I meditate, and that's how I get my wisdom." André smiled before he continued. "I left my home and family in Paris five years ago. For three years, I wandered in the Himalayan forests, seeking wisdom from yogi to yogi. I gained a lot and learnt a lot, but something was still missing. One fine day, I finally realized that I did not want to live in isolation. I did not want to renounce completely and become an ascetic." André paused for a moment and then added, "Then I met a yogi from Goa who turned my world around. I followed him to Goa. As soon as I put my foot on this land, I knew this was it! Now I live in this world but do not belong to it. I do not form attachments or have expectations of people or situations. I pray to Lord Shiva, and I am simply dancing in his creation. That's all I do." André's word were slow and precise in his tuneful French accent.

"Holy cow! You sound so out of this world, André. I feel completely enraptured," shouted Belinda.

"Boy, oh boy! I've got a lot to learn from you André," agreed Layla.

André beamed. "Okay now, *mes chéries*. Let's get prepared to go to the beach. It's a beautiful day."

"Where's the toilet, André?" asked Belinda.

"Aha! The toilet." André laughed. "Rosie! Could you please show the ladies the toilet?"

Rosie walked in with a metal container brimming with water and motioned for the girls to follow her. She walked them out of the house and onto a path created by trampling feet. They crossed a well around which a mother bathed her crying, soapy child. A dog barked at Rosie, but she warded it off with a stick. After another two minutes, they reached their destination: a raised platform with holes in it. Rosie explained to the girls in her broken English, and by pantomiming, that they needed to squat over the holes to do their business. There were only three walls around the toilets, which left the front open.

Belinda went in first; Layla stood in front of her to block her from view. As soon as Belinda was done, she was startled by a grunting noise coming from underneath the platform. André later explained to the girls the unique sanitation system of Anjuna. The pigs had their own passageway to reach underneath the platform. Whatever went through the holes was eaten by the pigs.

"Boy, oh boy! That's unique," exclaimed Layla in astonishment as she laughed with raised brows.

"Holy cow! Or rather, holy pig!" laughed Belinda.

Soon they were ready to leave the house. André handed a pink parasol to one and a purple parasol to the other. As they walked, twirling their parasols gently while resting them on their shoulders, they noticed tiny Goan houses with thatched roofs and stone walls scattered on little hillocks by the beach. A European woman lounged in a hammock in the front yard of her house under the shade of a tree. She lay bare-chested with closed eyes and fingers locked behind her head, revealing her unshaved armpits. An open book, turned upside down, rested on her navel. "She is Italian Sophia, our neighbour," commented André.

A man with shoulder-length brown hair and freckled cheeks sat under a tree, playing melodiously on his guitar. "He is Spanish Juan," noted André, waving at the man.

"Hola, hombre!" Juan said, waving back.

Layla and Belinda couldn't spot one local Goan lounging around as they walked to the beach. It seemed like the white hippies had invaded this beach, ushering all the locals out of the area. The only local Goans they could spot were the ones who owned chai shops or restaurants, and who worked in the houses of hippies.

Layla lifted the hem of her maxi to step over boulders that led to the sea shore. They strolled along the shore to reach the southern end of the beach where everyone gathered. As they approached closer, Layla and Belinda were awed to see around 150 people with tanned and naked bodies lying in the sun, playing, reading, dancing, and singing. They heard a group of guys cheering as they played badminton in the sun. "Whoa!" yelled Layla, sidestepping as a shuttle flew past her face. "Boy, oh boy! That was close." She exchanged glances with Belinda. They couldn't hold in their excitement in regards to what they were seeing.

"I love it!" yelled Belinda as she took off her dress and ran into the sea, followed by Layla. André joined the two.

Belinda and André were still playing in the ocean waves when Layla swam out. She spread her dress on the sand and lay on it with closed eyes to soak some sun, and she gradually nodded off. Belinda's giggles woke her up a little bit later. André and Belinda were rolling in the sand as he tickled her. "Stop!" she managed to say between guffaws. Tired of swimming and playing, André now lazily lay on the sand with Belinda lying beside him, her head resting on his arm. They dozed off for a few minutes before a female voice in a tuneful Italian accent woke them up.

"Ciao, amore!" called out Italian Sofia in her musical accent. She wore a swirly tulle skirt with a floppy hat. Her long, sandy-brown hair fell all over her pretty, pale face as she stooped over to look at André. Sofia, a former Italian model who'd once lived an upscale life in Rome, had given up her former yuppie lifestyle to live a free and natural life on the beaches of Goa.

"Hey, Sophia! How are you, *ma chérie*?" greeted André as Belinda lazily rolled over to the side, allowing André to sit up. Sophia kneeled over to give him a hug and a kiss. André introduced her to Layla and Belinda.

"Welcome to paradise, ladies" said Sophia as she gave the women a hug and a kiss each. "Are you coming to the party tonight?"

"Where is the party?" inquired André.

"At Handsome Leonardo's, of course. You don't know about it? Everybody has been waiting so anxiously to attend it."

"Oh, yeah! I remember him inviting me. Good that you reminded me. I'll be there for sure."

"See you there! Ciao, amore!" said Sophia with a kiss as she waved him goodbye.

"Okay, ladies, let's get going and get some rest if we want to enjoy the party tonight," said André excitedly, in anticipation of what was coming.

The three of them walked homewards, exchanging hugs and kisses and waving at the colourful people lounging around the beach. After having a warm lunch of Goan peas and coconut *pulao* (rice) prepared by Rosie, the three of them retired to their rooms for a siesta. Belinda slept in André's room that afternoon.

In the evening, Layla woke up to the sound of someone tapping on the door "Layla! Layla, wake up!" called Belinda from behind the door.

Layla jumped out of her bed and unlatched the door to let Belinda walk in. "Hey, you naughty thing! How was it?" prompted Layla with a sneaky grin as she nudged Belinda.

Belinda smiled mischievously and then announced, "Well, it was great!" She paused and added after a moment's reflection, "He is really cute, you know. He's kind, gentle, funny, and loving. I think I am falling for him." Belinda had a slow and mellow tone.

"Boy, oh boy! This missy is falling in love." She giggled and then added, "Do not forget that he is wise too."

"What do you mean?" grunted Belinda.

"Well, I am really happy for you Belinda. I agree that André is a great guy. Both of you look really cute together." Layla leaned over, held Belinda's hand, and said, "But do keep in mind what he told us the other day. He does not form attachments, so save yourself the hurt of getting too attached to him. Have fun with him, play with him, but try not to get too attached to him. Okey-dokey?"

"Sure, Layla" said Belinda, giving Layla a hug. "Now, let's hurry up and get dressed for the party. André is almost ready."

"I don't know why, but I am really excited about this party," Layla said.

"Okay, then. Let's get started!"

Layla and Belinda wore long, flowing, backless dresses. They sprinkled glitter in their hair and cleavage, and they put shimmer on their eyes and cheekbones. Belinda painted a butterfly on the top part of her right breast.

André walked out of his room wearing blue velvet flare pants and a front open blue silk vest embroidered in gold. His long blond hair accented his attire as he habitually flicked them to a side.

"Holy cow!" exclaimed Belinda, shaking her bangs as she whistled in admiration. André winked in response, and Layla chuckled. They were ready for the party.

André locked the door of his house and switched on his flashlight. Layla and Belinda hitched up their dresses, and the three started walking towards Handsome Leonardo's house. The full moon hung low over the ocean, creating a bright silvery pathway of light on water. They walked past the beach, meandered through a paddy field, crossed a ravine, and jumped over a few mounds to finally reach their destination.

"That must be it," Belinda said ecstatically as she pointed towards a house lit up with candles and lanterns, which were set amidst a garden of flowers. Light flickered through trees and bushes as if dancing to the sound of music that could be heard from a distance. As they edged closer to the house, they saw a racing-green convertible Aston Martin drive up the paved road; it parked beside the house and under a tree lit up with lanterns. The light of the lanterns fell directly on the face of the young man who stepped out of it. He had the looks of a Greek hero: big brown eyes, a chiselled jawline, sharp nose, and gelled black hair long enough to cover his nape. He wore a groovy Edwardian-style velvet trim half-sleeve black jacket with a white fringe shirt and black flare pants. Layla's heart skipped a beat at the sight of him. He opened the wooden gate, walked inside, and disappeared in the crowd. Despite his magnetic charm, there was something odd about the guy. He didn't seem to fit in. He seemed foreign amidst the glittering and sparkling tie-dyed crowd.

André unlatched the wooden gate, and the three of them walked inside the yard of the house. A group of hippies sang and played music with guitar, drums, saxophone, and flutes. People danced untamed, wearing silk and tassels. Dressed in glitters, sparkles, funky masks, and with painted faces, they lolled on mattresses arranged in small semicircles covered with scarlet satin sheets and cushy bolsters. Candles flickered in decorative candle holders lighting up the area.

André led the girls inside the house, which was filled with more sparkly people. People lounged on silk-covered mattresses placed around Persian rugs. They tinkled their wine glasses and beer mugs as they walked past each other. Rajasthani tapestries, flower work embroidery, and decorative brass mirrors adorned the walls. The soothing aroma of jasmine oil that was lit in burners in the corners of the house, was creating an intoxicating effect. Amidst decorative lanterns and candles sat Handsome Leonardo and his Spanish wife, proffering lines of cocaine. Leonardo, a tall and handsome man with long, streaky hair tied neatly in a ponytail, wore green velvet bellbottoms and a ruffled tux shirt. Isabella, his pretty and dainty wife, had shiny black hair and green eyes, and she wore a long and slinky halter gown with glitter in her hair and shimmer on her eyes. Loaded in gems and stones, she tinkled and jingled from head to toe.

"Ciao, Bello! How are you?" greeted Leonardo with open arms, giving André a hug.

"Doing great, Leo. You've got a great party going. I love it," commented André with admiration.

"Grazi, Bello." Leonardo gave a smile and then said in his strong Italian accent, "Care for some coke?"

"No, thank you! I will light a chillum instead."

"Sure, sure! Go right ahead."

"Leo, meet my friends Belinda and Layla. They just arrived yesterday. It's their first time in Goa."

"It is very nice to meet you ladies. Welcome to paradise," Leonardo said, bowing down in a very gentlemanly manner. "Please feel free to help yourself with some drinks, coke, hash, acid—whatever you like." He pointed to wherever everything was.

Layla and Belinda thanked him and moved on. They felt ecstatic about being where they were. Layla maintained her composure, but Belinda couldn't control her ear-to-ear grin. André left the girls to join the "Bam Bhole" group sitting huddled together in a circle in the backyard to light a chillum.

"Care for some coke?" Belinda asked Layla with a wink.

"Are you kidding, Belinda? You know that coke is not my thing. Pot is about all that I can handle. I think I'll just stick to some beer today. You go ahead. Enjoy!" said Layla with a slight smirk.

"Okay," said Belinda as she moved to the group seated on mattresses around Leonardo and Isabella, squeezing in between them.

Leonardo held a straw full of acid over the tongue of a long-haired blonde woman, and he tapped it as he noticed Belinda squeezed by his side. "Here you are, Bella. It is so nice to have you with us. Here, try some coke." Leonardo picked up and offered her a gilded mirror with fine lines of cocaine on it. Isabella handed her a rolled-up 100-rupee note.

"Thank you," whispered Belinda as she took a long sniff and reclined back.

"Hello there, lady!" Layla heard a deep, smooth male voice whisper in her ear as she puttered in a corner, enjoying the show. She turned around, and there stood her knight in shining armour. He was the dapper guy who had appeared out of the racing-green Aston Martin. There was something about this man Layla found utterly attractive. He was not at all her type and seemed like he belonged to the straight world that Layla had forsaken years ago. But still he made her blush—something that had not happened to her in years. She had had many teenage crushes, like all girls did, as well as a couple of flings here and there, but the fire she felt for him, she had never felt for any guy other than Jim Morrison. Jim was still her first love, but this man would be her second.

"Hi!" replied Layla with a smile, attempting to conceal her feelings.

"Can I help you with a drink, please? What would you like to have, lady?" said the man in a slight British accent. It wasn't pure British, but a mix of Indian and British.

"Thank you! Well, I think I'll just have some beer or, um, maybe some wine."

"Let's walk outside to the bar, and you can decide," offered the man.

The two walked outside to the yard, where the bar was set up. Layla decided upon a glass of sparkling white wine, and the man had a beer. The two stood under a tree lit up with lanterns.

"If you don't mind me asking," said Layla with a bit of hesitation, "you don't exactly look like a part of the crowd."

The man laughed and then stated, "Well, I am not!" He paused, smiled, and clarified. "I am not a hippie, and I don't live in a hut on Anjuna beach. My name is Gary, and I am a friend of Leonardo's. He and his wife are regular visitors to my hotel. We share a common passion, of horses. That's how we became friends. He accompanied me a couple of times to Jodhpur and Poona for horse racing and polo. He is quite passionate about the sport, you know. He owns a horse farm back in Sicily. He invited me to his party, and that's why I am here."

A feathered woman in purple samba costume brushed against him to order her drink. "One martini, please," she called out.

Layla and Gary sidestepped to continue with the conversation.

"Oh, nice! That explains it," said Layla with a nervous chuckle. "Nice meeting you, Gary. I am Layla. I and my friend Belinda arrived in Goa yesterday. We have already fallen in love with the place."

"It happens that Goa is a magical place, and it makes people fall in love," said Gary with a romantic smile.

Layla giggled as a man in a gold disco shirt bobbed up and down beside her. "Looks-wise, um, I would guess you look sort of Greek or Italian. But you have a bit of a British accent. I am wondering about your background."

"I am a purebred Indian. I owe my slight British accent to my university years spent in London, studying hotel management."

"Nice. You said you own a hotel here in Goa?"

"Yes, I do. That's why I live here. My parents live in Chandigarh, a small city close to Delhi. Would you like to see my hotel one day? Maybe tomorrow, if you are free?"

"Sure, why not?" Layla readily consented, jumping at the opportunity as she inched closer to him.

The band started playing Dean Martin's "Sway," and the glittered and bedecked couples filled up the dance floor for some passionate, sexy dancing. Gary offered Layla his hand, and the two stepped on the dance floor, engaging in a sassy rumba. Gary hummed along with the song as he swung Layla in his arms.

> Like a flower bending in the breeze,
>
> Bend with me, sway with ease.
>
> When we dance, you have a way with me.
>
> Stay with me, sway with me ...

André, Belinda, Leonardo, and Isabella joined in the dance too. The full moon peeked through the swaying palms, lending its silvery shimmer to the dancers as they swung and spun under the diamond-studded sky until the wee hours of the morning.

Chapter 9

Till the Heavens Stop the Rain

Now I'm gonna love you,
Till the heavens stop the rain.
I'm gonna love you,
Till the stars fall from the sky for you and I.

— Jim Morrison

Layla woke up to a gentle *tipper-tapper* of the rain falling on the thatched roof of the house. She was in love and couldn't get the smile off her face.

Suddenly, she heard a knock on the door. "Madam, coffee is ready," called out Rosie. After quickly freshening up, Layla walked down the creaky wooden stairs to where André and Belinda sat around a small table, sipping coffee.

"Hey! You had a lot of fun last night, didn't you?" prompted Belinda with a grin as Layla joined them.

"Yeah! It was a lot of fun." Layla smiled with a downcast glance, seeming a bit bashful.

"Who was that groovy guy, huh?" asked Belinda curiously, leaning over to Layla and stroking her sleeve.

"Dream lover!" Layla grinned. "I'll introduce you both to him—he's coming to pick me up today."

"Holy cow! That was fast!" Belinda broke up in a roaring laughter, and André chuckled. "But he's so straight!" exclaimed Belinda in a strained voice as she frowned.

"I know, but I like him," announced Layla with a careless shrug.

"Good for you," said Belinda, giggling some more.

"He seems fantastic, *ma chérie*! I have been to his hotel a few times. I agree with Belinda that he is kind of straight, but I believe you will have a good time with him," remarked André. He gave a wink and a thumbs-up.

Layla smiled and kissed them both before sprinting to her room to get dressed. She wore a purple floral maxi with a tube top and decorated a purple orchid in her blonde hair, which swayed down to her bare waist. She pirouetted over to the window to see whether he was there. *Not yet!* Everything seemed surreal to her as she sat on the window sill. The maiden drawing water from the well, the little boy watching the chickens peck the ground, the cawing of the crow that whizzed past her, the trotting dog that contentedly whisked its tail, the fragrance of the orchid in her hair, and the rainbow that accompanied the earthy scent after a shower. She wondered whether there was going to be a pot of gold at the end of the rainbow. She smiled and pinched herself.

Soon Gary was walking towards the house with a bunch of red roses in his hand. He wore Morrison-like aviator glasses, a white cotton shirt, royal Stewart Tartan pants, and black-and-white leather loafers. He stood by the open doorway and gently tapped on the open door. André ushered him in after introducing himself.

"Hi there!" called out Layla gleefully as she darted down the stairs and welcomed him with a hug and a kiss. Gary handed her the roses. "Ah, thank you. They are so beautiful!" she exclaimed.

Belinda walked in the room when Layla was hurriedly yet artfully arranging the flowers in the vase. "Holy cow! That's so cool! Red roses! I love that!" she said, clasping her hands together as she walked over to Gary and introduced herself with a hug.

"Would you like to drink something, or shall we?" offered Layla in a rather hurried tone.

"No! Let's go," answered Gary with a smile. Layla picked up her floppy hat and waved goodbye, and off they went.

"We will have to walk a little distance to the paved road where I have parked my car," said Gary as they went along a grassy path. A group of piglets grunted and then scurried away at their step. Layla hitched up her dress as they walked through a part of a paddy field followed by clambering over a few boulders. Gary jumped atop a boulder and offered his hand to pull her up towards him, holding her in a gentle embrace. They stood still and locked for a few moments before meandering through a lush ravine, where they stopped. Beams of sunlight breached the lush green canopy as Gary held Layla in his arms. He looked deep into her intense blue eyes, caressed her rosy lips, and then kissed her. Raindrops still rested on the green tree leaves that gently brushed against her face. After going up and over a few mounds, Layla could spot the green Aston Martin parked by the roadside.

He opened the car door for her, and soon they were driving down a narrow, winding road shrouded by a thick cover of the palms.

"How far is your hotel?" asked Layla, glancing at him.

"It's about a 20-minute drive. In Calangute," answered Gary, tilting his head slightly sideways.

"My father owns hotels across the United States, but I hardly have any relationship left with my parents now. I write to them here and there, send them postcards of places that I travel. They are nice enough to deposit my monthly allowance in the bank, and that's about it," Layla said in a monotone with a blank gaze resting on the road ahead.

"What went wrong with your relationship? The lifestyle that you chose, I presume?" said Gary, turning his head to steal a quick look at her.

"Yes, you are right. They don't agree with my ways. My father wanted me to get a degree in hotel management and take care of his business. But that's just not my cup of tea. I want more from life." She glanced at him with a smile.

"What if a straight guy like your dad falls in love with you and wants you to join his world?"

"No way! If he truly loves me, he will let me live my life my way, and we can still marry and stay in love," Layla replied with a smile.

"I understand," said Gary, throwing her a loving glance and smiling at her sweet stubbornness.

He propelled his shiny green Aston Martin into the curvy driveway of his beachside hotel, the Sun Palace. A turbaned valet parking attendant first saluted and then walked towards the car, bowing to his *sahib* (master). Gary handed him the car keys with a smile and then walked Layla in, holding her gently by the waist. Two women attendants dressed in fancy Goan outfits approached Layla. One placed a garland of marigolds around her neck, and the other put a red dot on her forehead. "Thank you," said Layla gleefully. The sight of the hotel overwhelmed her. The hotel sprawled over 15 acres of lush, green gardens. The front-open, central dome where they stood provided a spectacular view of the turquoise waters of the Arabian Sea. The dome was embellished with brass-framed paintings of the royals, depicting old-world architecture in its carved wooden and marble panels. The corners were fragrant with rose petals floating in water-filled, fancy brass containers. The hotel was a castle situated in tropical paradise.

"Gurveer Sahib, the table is set for you two at the ocean bar," said a turbaned waiter, bowing down.

"Gurveer? You name is Gurveer?" asked Layla straining her eyebrows.

"Yes! Gurveer Singh Sandhu officially, but I go by Gary amongst family and friends," explained Gary.

"Ah! Nice to know that." Layla smiled while glancing up at him.

The two walked towards the hotel bar situated right by the ocean. They snuggled together in a circular love seat and listened to the soothing sound of the ocean waves crashing against the rocky beach, mixed with the romantic jazz music playing in the bar. Gary's right arm was wrapped gently around her shoulder, stroking her side.

A turbaned waiter in a long tunic held a notepad and a pen. He bowed to Gary "What can I get for you, Sir?"

"A cold house draft for me. What would you like, Layla?" asked Gary.

"Glass of white wine, please" she said to the waiter.

They sipped their drinks and nibbled on cheese and peanuts while they shared their little secrets and laughed.

"Come, let me show you my little abode," said Gary. The two walked towards the fenced, private area of the hotel. A little house shrouded in flowers lay hidden in the lush green. Gary unlocked the door, and the two stepped inside a majestic living room decorated with brass-framed painting of horses and bronze artefacts. On the main wall of the living room hung a portrait of a turbaned officer in army uniform embellished with medals and stars. On both sides of the portrait hung decorative shields and spears. Layla stood still on the Persian rug to look at the detailed portrait of the officer.

"That's my father. He's a brigadier in the Indian Army. He wanted me to join the Indian Army too, but I wanted to be in the hospitality industry," Gary said with a smile. He continued after a moment's pause. "My grandfather and forefathers were all landlords. We own a vast land in Punjab—that's a state in Northern India. After completing my hotel management studies in London, I requested my dad sell a piece of that land to buy me land over here in Goa, so I could set up a hotel here. That's how I am here." Gary smiled, and Layla smiled back. "Come, let me show you my room. We have two bedrooms in this little house, one for me and one for my family, which visits quite often."

He led her by the hand into his bedroom. It was a neat, fancy room with floor to ceiling windows that opened to a flower-laden walk-out patio. The room had framed portraits of Gary horse racing and playing polo. Family pictures in small frames adorned a side wall. There was a black-and-white picture of a young couple riding horses. "That's my mom and dad when they were young," he pointed out.

"Boy, oh boy! They make a gorgeous couple. Your dad is very handsome, and your mom is very beautiful," commented Layla.

"She is very beautiful—but not as beautiful as you, Layla," he murmured, stroking her cheek gently. "Want some wine?"

"Yes, sure!" she answered as she blushed. Gary poured two glasses of white wine from his small corner bar and then bent over to where a record player was placed. He flipped through neatly shelved rows of album covers and selected "Romantic Jazz." He slid the round disc out of its cover, held it by the edges, and slipped it into place. As he placed the record arm on the disc, music started to play. He walked over to Layla and offered her a glass of wine, and then the two toasted with arms intertwined. They placed the glasses on the side table for a slow dance. They swayed softly, locked in each other's arms. Time stood still for Layla. She tightened her grip around him for a moment, just to make sure all was real and not a dream.

Gary was lost in thought too, wondering how quickly the world had changed around him. Till yesterday, he didn't even know that Layla existed, and today she seemed like the focal point of his life. He was head over heels in love with her. He didn't want her to leave—ever. He bent over and softly placed his lips on hers, and they kissed.

As they kissed, a horse neighed. "That's Top Gun cheering as we kiss," Gary noted, chuckling.

"You have horses here?" asked Layla in astonishment.

"A couple of them back in the stable. Top Gun and Cairo. You want to ride?" asked Gary.

"Yes, I would love to!" answered Layla.

"Okay, then. Let's get changed. I think you will fit into my cousin's jodhpurs and riding boots. My cousin, Jasmine, visits me quite often, and we go riding, so she left her horse riding gear here. It's hanging in that wardrobe. Let me grab it for you." Gary dashed towards the cupboard.

Soon Gary and Layla were changed into breeches, chaps, and riding boots. Gary threw her a helmet as he whistled. "You look like Maharani Gayitri Devi in this gear," he complimented.

"Are you talking about the Indian princess?" Layla asked.

He replied, "Yes! The beautiful Indian princess who is a fashion icon. She was listed amongst the most beautiful women in the world by *Vogue* magazine in 1960. You are a replica of her, but with blue eyes and long blonde hair." Layla giggled.

They walked towards the stables. Gary saddled up a horse and helped Layla mount it. He mounted behind her, and with his arms wrapped around her, he held the reins as they galloped towards the beach. They rode by the sandy beach in the fading light of the setting sun, which was slowly disappearing behind the emerald ocean, leaving the sky aglow in a mix of orange, pink, and purple.

The waves tickled the shore in a soothing rhythm as the horse galloped. They rode along scenic green country trails and winding paths lined by coconut palms. Soon it was dark, and they rode back to the stable. Gary and Layla dismounted from the horse. Gary stroke his mane and his glistening coat as he whispered, "Good boy, Top Gun,"

They showered and changed. Gary gifted Layla a backless red gown he had picked up from the hotel's gift shop for a special evening that he had planned for her. He walked her to the private area of the beach, where a special table was set for them under a pagoda of red roses. They wined and dined on a candlelit table while a band played just for them. After dinner, they walked by the shore, hand in hand, to a remote end where they could not be seen or heard. They lay on the sand under a blanket of stars, locked in each other's arms. The moon hung low, the ocean shimmered in its silvery light, the waves splashed against the shore, and the seagulls called as they consummated their love.

Chapter 10

I'm Only Sleeping

Please don't wake me, no don't shake me.
Leave me where I am, I'm only sleeping.
Everybody seems to think I'm lazy.
I don't mind, I think they're crazy,
Running everywhere at such speed,
Till they find there's no need ... there's no need.

—*John Lennon and Paul McCartney*

The next morning, Gary dropped Layla off at home. "I'm home! Belinda, André, where are you guys?" she called out.

André walked out of his room with a displeased look on his face "Belinda is not home. We went to a friend's house yesterday afternoon for a little get-together. Belinda hasn't been back since. She was doing line after line of cocaine. I tried to pull her out of there, but she wouldn't budge. She must be still lying there in a heap." He grunted, throwing his arms up in the air.

"Who is this friend of yours, and could you take me to his house, please, André?" said Layla with a worried look on her face.

"Sure. He is Spanish Juan, known for always dispensing free cocaine to the ones he takes a fancy to," he grumpily informed her.

The two trampled through a narrow path shrouded by trees and then went over a few mounds. André stood atop a mound and pointed. "That's Juan's house." On a small hillock perched a small, two-storey stone house with a thatched roof. Trance music could be heard from a distance. As they walked inside the house, which was filled with marijuana fog, they saw about 15 people lounging around on an Afghani rug of the living room against the backdrop of a brass-framed portrait of Elvis Presley adorning the central wall. A garland of marigolds hung around the portrait frame. A cluster of people sat around a *chabudai*, a Japanese-style, short-legged table, placed near the kitchen. A few hung around the back porch. Silk saris, embroidered wall hangings, and Tibetan paintings adorned the walls.

In the middle of the Afghani rug sat Spanish Juan, holding court. He held a glass coaster in his hand, and with a sharp razor blade, he made fine lines of white cocaine powder. He recounted tales of adventure and gusto as he chopped cocaine. Bright red freckles spattered his cheeks, and they glistened as he gave a toothy grin that accompanied his jokes.

Belinda lay down with her head resting on a burgundy silk cushion. Her legs rested on a lanky, long-haired man's lap, who sat beside her.

"Hey, hombre! Come on in, man. I was waiting for you," greeted Spanish Juan in a cheerful voice.

"Hey, Juan. Meet Layla, Belinda's friend," André said. "I hope Belinda is doing okay?" He had concern on his face.

"No worries, friend. She is fine. She is having fun. We danced all night under the stars. She was super excited, totally wired, hyper, and buzzing—too much coke, man. She just fell asleep," said Spanish Juan in a nonchalant way. Then he added, "Hey, hombre!

Come smoke a chillum, man. Have fun. The Bam Bhole group is in the back porch under the mango tree. And Layla, come join us. What would you like? Some grass, coke, smack, acid? Whatever you prefer. Please feel free to mingle and snort." Spanish Juan grinned.

"Thanks, Juan, but let me check on Belinda first," said Layla.

André walked indifferently to the back porch to light a chillum. "Bam Bam Bhole," Layla heard André bellow a moment later.

She meandered her way through sitting and lying bodies and kneeled next to Belinda. She shook, rocked, and jolted her. "Belinda, wake up!" she called out numerous times before Belinda opened her bloodshot eyes with dilated pupils. "Are you okay?" whispered Layla

"Yes, yes. Um, I am fine," mumbled Belinda as she woke up, squeezing her temples.

"You are fine, I agree—but not fine, lady. I think you will need some heroin. You sniffed too much coke yesterday," Spanish Juan said, laughing. "You just wouldn't listen. A sniff of heroin will make it all better, I tell you. Heroin cures the cocaine comedown like nothing else. Then you go home and get some sound sleep, okay?"

"Yes! I do need something. I can't move a limb otherwise," groaned Belinda.

Spanish Juan extended his hand and offered Belinda a glass block with finely arranged lines of brown powder and a rolled-up bill. Belinda took hold of the bill and sniffed the powder up her nose. The heroin seeped into her bloodstream, and as soon as it reached her brain, her body eased and her nerves relaxed. Leaning back, she sank deep into a cushion placed against a yielding wall, enjoying the intense surge of euphoria. Her skin flushed warmly as she reclined with her head lolled back.

"Let her relax for a little bit, before you take her home," suggested Spanish Juan. "How about you? Care for something little?"

"Yes, sure, while I am waiting for Belinda. Um, I'll try that fancy glass bong you have in that corner. Thank you," said Layla, walking over to the corner where the bong sat. She sat down comfortably, rested her back against the cushioned wall, and placed her lips firmly around the opening of the vertical pipe containing water. An attached side bowl contained marijuana mixed with tobacco. She relaxed as she savoured a lungful of marijuana smoke with closed eyes. Her limbs eased, and her thoughts drifted to Gary. She was so in love with him. Her world had suddenly turned so beautiful, so dreamy. She loved her life, she loved Gary, she loved Goa, and she loved André and Belinda ... Belinda? Something worried her about Belinda. Something didn't seem right. Belinda was too reckless, impulsive, hasty—a complete daredevil. Goa seemed a bit dangerous for her. Belinda had to hold her horses if she wanted to enjoy her life in Goa. Layla felt responsible for Belinda's life. After all, who else was there for her? Layla had to take charge; she had to guide her right.

Even after a half an hour, Belinda was still not ready to go. Layla requested André carry her home, and he did. He carried her on his shoulder, walked her home, and placed her on a mattress. He turned around to face Layla and lashed out in his French accent. "She could die like this! Does she know that? She needs to have some control over what she snorts, and how much. A dear friend of mine just died last month from snorting too much coke overnight—over a *single* night. Goa has too many cases of hippies dying of overdoses. We have found dead bodies washed ashore on the beach in the morning. They snort too much, jump in, and don't come out. We have not come here to die. Have we?" His tone softened after a moment's pause. "I care about Belinda. She is sweet, bubbly, and vivacious. I want her to have fun. But I want her to consume only what she can handle. And if she cannot handle it, she must *not* consume." He shrugged his shoulders. "I smoke hash too, but I keep a check on how much I smoke, and I have control over what I consume. If we lose control once we start, it means we have a serious problem. It's a problem that must be addressed before it's too late. We came to Anjuna to live in a free, peaceful, and loving environment, not to die in it. Please have a talk with your friend once she is feeling fine." He sighed and mumbled with a downcast glance, "I am sorry if I blurted out too much."

"Oh, no, that's absolutely fine. Just shows how much you care," whispered Layla as she walked over to André and hugged him tenderly.

Belinda slept through the day and woke up at night. Sleep helped her recover, though she still did not feel at her best. Layla took her for a stroll by the beach. As they walked down the sandy beach, Layla talked to Belinda about her well-being. She explained how important it was for her to stay healthy and in control of her situation so that they could enjoy their lives in Goa. She also talked about André and how much he cared for her. "Let's both stay healthy and enjoy life. Life is beautiful, and all is perfect. Let's not ruin it," urged Layla, holding Belinda by the shoulders.

"Yes, you are right," murmured Belinda, giving Layla a hug.

Days rolled into weeks, and weeks turned into months. Layla and Belinda rented a beautiful beachside bungalow close to André's house. They spent long, sunny days lounging on the beach and danced all night under a starlit sky. Life was one long party—no schedule to follow, no chores, no obligations. No one cared about the exact time of the day; all they did was follow the sun to figure out their mornings, afternoons, and nights. No one cared about what day it was because every day was a Sunday for them.

Layla and Gary were together every day and every night, either at her house or his. Their love blossomed under the Goan moon. With every sunrise, they grew closer to each other.

Belinda and André were going through an up-and-down relationship. They were in love, but Belinda was becoming extremely hard to handle. Her wild, untamed spirit didn't accept commandments.

André was invariably taking care of her, making sure that she was not consuming more than she could handle. There were days when they wouldn't leave each other's side, and there were days when they couldn't even look at one another. André gave up on her many times in frustration, but eventually he came back.

No one at Anjuna cared about what month it was, but when it was December, they all knew. The beaches filled up as hippies trickled in from everywhere. There were long beach parties that continued for days on end. One fine December evening, as Layla and Belinda were getting ready for a beach party, Gary showed up on his motorbike. He waved at Layla to come down as she peered through her bedroom window.

"I want to take you for a ride, Layla," he said with a romantic smile as he handed her a single red rose while still seated on the motorbike. Layla beamed, flung a leg over, and climbed behind him. They drove off on a winding dirt road under the dense foliage of the coconut palms. They weaved through flowery bushes with chattering birds that flew away as they drove closer. They headed over a few sandy mounds and then reached the paved road. His brown suede open jacket fluttered in the rushing wind as Layla wrapped her arms around his bare midriff. He looked dapper with his aviator sunglasses as she watched him ride in the side mirror of the motorbike. They were driving towards his hotel. Soon he drove onto the passageway that led to his house and parked his bike on a side. As they walked inside the house, he gifted her a beautiful scarlet gown and asked her to change into it.

"What for?" she asked.

"There's a little party I would like to take you to tonight," he answered.

As Layla walked out wearing a scarlet halter gown, Gary was already changed into a black tuxedo with white fringe shirt. "Boy, oh boy!" exclaimed Layla as she whistled at the sight of him. He did likewise, and they walked out arm in arm. Gary opened the car door for her, and they drove a little distance on the paved road. Soon they were driving up a pebbled path leading up a lush green rolling hill. He parked his green Aston Martin at the very top.

"Where's the party?" she asked with a confused look on her face.

"We are running a bit early for the party, so I thought I'd just show you my favourite spot before we drive ahead. It is called the Sunset Point. Do you like this place?" he asked with a smile.

"I love it! It is so beautiful!" exclaimed Belinda as she surveyed the scenery. From the top she could view the turquoise Arabian Sea in all its glory. The hill was covered with majestic palms standing tall, and rows of bright flowers circled around tall trees that bordered the edges of the flat surface of the hill. Down below, large waves were crashing against the rocky shore. All was aglow in the fading orange rays of the setting sun going down the horizon. A flight of sea gulls screamed as they flew high in circles above the sea. Birds chirped around bushes.

Gary turned towards Layla, gently held her hands, and looked intensely into her blue eyes, which matched the colour of the ocean. His lips bore the semblance of a smile. Suddenly he bent down on one knee, opened a small red case holding a shining diamond, and said, "Will you marry me, Layla?"

Tears of joy streamed down her cheeks as she leaped on him with a "Yes!" knocking him off his step.

"Whoa!" he shouted joyously, trying to regain control as he swung her around in his arms with a wide smile across his face. As they kissed, sparkling fireworks lit up the sky in a dance of colours. Trees and bushes lit up with fairy lights, and a music band, previously hidden from view, started playing celebratory music. Gary held Layla in his arms, and they swayed to the music, overwhelmed with joy. Belinda, André, and a few of their close friends appeared from behind the bushes, clapping and whistling while dressed in glitter and shimmer. Belinda swayed in Gary's arms filled with wonder, her joy knowing no bounds. Within minutes, a dance floor was set up on-site, and they danced into the night, lit up with shimmering red lights, under a star-speckled sky as the moon shone down merrily upon them.

Gary slept over at Layla's house that night. The next afternoon, Layla suggested that they walked to Pete's Restaurant for lunch. They walked hand in hand on the sand and then meandered through a grove of coconut palms. A water buffalo wallowing in a mud-hole stopped a moment to look at them as they crossed a nearby swamp. They walked through a ravine and then entered a garden of flowers, amidst which stood the tiny restaurant. They walked up the steps to the wide-open front porch. Layla and Gary chose a wobbly wooden table set up in a corner. The rest of the tables were occupied by half-naked hippie foreigners with tanned skins decorated with tattoos. Most of them were barefoot with salt residue still resting on their bodies after a dip in the ocean. The front area of the restaurant beneath the porch was perpetually occupied by a group of hippies smoking chillum. A voice shouting "Bam Bhole" and "Bam Shankar" could be heard every few minutes.

Gary and Layla sat browsing through the menu hung on the wall. A young boy with side-parted short hair and dressed in shorts and a vest approached them for their order.

"Baked fish and potatoes with rosemary and garlic for me, please," ordered Gary.

"Steamed salmon and vegetable rice for me, please," said Layla.

As the boy left with the order, Layla held Gary's hand and said, "I love you a lot, Gary. I feel I am the happiest and luckiest woman on earth to have you as my would-be husband. But you know me well, and you know the life that I have chosen. I love Anjuna and my life here. Look around. You see these people? I am one of them. The only difference is that today I have a man in my life who is *not* one of them." she paused and added, "All I want to say is that I hope you will not have any problem with my chosen lifestyle. I will make every effort to mingle in your world as your wife, but you must know that at heart, I will stay a flower child. I will forever stay true to you, but you must know that the traditional lifestyle is just not for me. I hope you will understand, support me, and accept me as I am."

"Yes, Love" said Gary, stroking her cheek. "I love you and accept you just as you are, and I do not want to change a thing about you. I will accompany you to the Anjuna parties, if you wish. I will also accompany you to the communal sunset whenever you wish. You are free to live any way you want to live—as long as you stay true to me." He gave a wink and a grin. Layla chuckled. "So, are we all clear and done?" he asked while holding her hand.

"Yes!" said Layla with a grin.

"Now, my love, may I seek your permission to introduce you to my family?"

"Yes, of course!" said Layla with a smile.

"For that, we will have to fly to Chandigarh in a day or two. I have already told my parents about you, and they are very excited to meet you. Actually, I have told them that I have already married you," he announced

"What? Wow!" exclaimed Layla, breaking out in a fit of laughter. "Boy, oh boy!" she uttered as she mellowed down and placed her hand on her chest.

Gary smiled and lovingly held her hand, placing his forehead against hers. They looked deep into each other's eyes, and the diamond on her ring finger sparkled as they kissed.

Chapter 11

Oh, My Love

Oh, my love, for the first time in my life,
My eyes are wide open.
Oh, my love, for the first time in my life,
My eyes can see.

—John Lennon

Layla and Gary flew to Delhi the next afternoon. Layla was dressed more conventionally this time, in blue denim bellbottoms and a cream cowl-neck sweater. She walked out of the gates of the airport holding onto Gary's arm. "Brr," she muttered, clenching his arm as she felt the chill of the cold air swipe across her face.

Sohan Singh, the chauffeur who had come to pick the two up from Delhi airport, glided towards them with folded palms. "Sat Sri Akal, Sahib and Madam," he greeted the two with a bow and a wide smile, happy to see his sahib's beautiful bride.

"Sat Sri Akal," they replied with a smile. As Sohan Singh turned his back, Gary flashed Layla a thumbs-up for her good work in pronouncing the greeting. Layla winked back with a smirk. Before coming, Gary had prepared Layla on how to meet and greet the Punjabi people.

Sohan Singh rushed to pick their baggage and led them to a shiny black Jaguar. He opened the car door, and the two slid inside. Soon they were on their way to Chandigarh. Cars, buses, and trucks crawled on the highway, blasting horns. Not much of the outside noise could be heard inside the rolled-up windows of the black Jag. John Lennon's "Oh My Love" played softly in the car as Layla rested her head gently on Gary's shoulder, intertwined her arm in his, and held his hand. He caressed her hair as she dreamt with open eyes.

Four hours flew by in no time, and then they were cruising down the wide and open roads of Chandigarh, shrouded by trees on either side, the thick foliage forming a leafy canopy overhead for the cars to drive through. The setting sun cast an orange haze above the horizon, lighting up the evening sky just before twilight. Sohan Singh drove through a narrow street lined with gated mansions, and he parked in front of a wide-open gate decorated with marigolds. He walked out and opened the car door for Gary and Layla. As Layla stepped out, she saw two finely-dressed women lined on one side of the gate and a tall, bearded, handsome man with an elegant woman on the other side of the gate.

"They are lined here to greet your arrival into the family and to bless you with some customary rituals," Gary whispered in Layla's ear as he smiled. Layla had already gone through the family album in Goa, and this made the guessing easy. Layla recognised the tall and handsome *cut-surd* (a Sikh man with trimmed hair and beard) and his beautiful wife as Gary's parents. The young girl on the other side of the gate would be Jasmine, Gary's cousin, whose horse riding gear Layla had been wearing in Goa. The woman beside her was probably her mother, Gary's aunt, his father's sister.

A copper vessel was placed on one side of the gate, brimming with mustard oil. Gary's mother, a fair and green-eyed woman, dressed in a pink silk *salwar kameez* (Indian dress) and *phulkari* (an embroidered flower work shawl), walked forward with a silver glass of water in her hand and asked Layla to lightly kick down the copper vessel with her bare right foot. Layla took off her shoes and then gently kicked the vessel. The mustard oil spilled to the side, and as beckoned, Layla walked in with Gary by her side. The family and the attendants showered rose petals on them as they walked in. A *dholi* (drummer) dressed in traditional Punjabi, brightly-coloured attire started beating the double-headed drum, a *dhol,* that hung around his nape down to his stomach. Gary's mother circled a glass of water thrice around Layla's head and then placed it gently on her lips, requesting she drink from it. Once done drinking, Gary's mother hugged her tight and kissed her on both cheeks and her forehead, cupping her face between her palms. "She is so beautiful Gary, more than you had mentioned!" his mother exclaimed joyously. Gary nudged Layla playfully, reminding her of her lessons, and the two bent down and touched his mother's feet. She blessed them by placing her palm on their heads.

Next, they walked towards Gary's father and touched his feet. He hugged, kissed, and blessed them. "Welcome home, my daughter! May God bless you two," he said lovingly. Jasmine and Gary's aunt (*bhua ji),* wearing similar *phulkaris* as Gary's mother, were the next to hug, kiss, and welcome Layla. The rest of the staff, consisting of chauffeur Sohan Singh, cook Bali Ram, and gardener Kashi Ram, steepled their palms together and bowed down respectfully.

Amidst the cheery giggles and the guffaws, Gary and the family walked Layla inside the house, as ecstatic as they could be. Gary walked Layla through the mansion with sprawling gardens and finally showed her their room, decorated all over with flowers. Their bed was covered in a canopy of red roses. Layla was overjoyed and enthralled to be a part of this warm family. Her throat tightened, and her eyes brimmed with tears of joy as she hugged Gary.

After Layla and Gary freshened and changed, the family lounged on wicker chairs set up in a circle around a bonfire, lit up in the lush green front lawn of the house. Bright yellow and orange flames flickered in the cool breeze, lending their glow to the faces seated around it. Noticing Layla shiver in the crisp December cold, Gary's mother gently draped a pashmina shawl around her shoulders. Layla smiled with a thank-you. Gary's father, wearing a warm woollen gown over his pyjama suit, poured drinks along with Gary: scotch on the rocks for men, red wine for the ladies. His salt-and-pepper beard was trimmed, and his short hair was combed straight back, lending him a noble look. Gary had told Layla he did not wear his turban at all times, only occasionally.

Gary's mother, a fine-mannered and sophisticated lady, daintily sipped on her wine. She tied a low bun on her nape, and her jet-black hair had one wide grey streak in the middle, combed to a side. A diamond nose pin shimmered in her Roman nose. She wore a Coco Chanel pyjama suit and a woollen gown over it. Gary's aunt was another elegant lady, tall and fair but of a quiet demeanour. She too tied a low bun over her nape and mostly smiled. Jasmine, a tall, pretty, dusky, and sporty girl of 20, was a bubble of energy, high spirits, and zest. She was also an incessant talker.

"Gary *veer* [brother], this is not right. How could you get married without your family by your side? Now you have to redo the whole thing again for us, the traditional way. I have to dance on your wedding, *yaar* [friend]," Jasmine said in a high-pitched voice with animated gesticulation.

"Actually, I put a ring on her finger, and according to me, that is a wedding. But in case you all want to do something elaborate, I am in for it," said Gary with a smile. Then he turned towards Layla and said, "What do you say, Layla?"

"You all have already done so much for me. I am running short of words to express my happiness and delight," Layla said with dewy eyes. Then she added, "Whatever you all decide, I am in for it."

"Yay!" shouted Jasmine joyfully.

Gary's parents, seated on either side of Layla, leaned towards her and hugged her. "We are very happy to have you in our family, *beta ji* . We had been looking for a perfect bride for Gary for such a long time, but Gary wouldn't listen. He would say, 'Mom and Dad, please don't worry about me. I will find my own love. You leave it to me.' So we left it to him. Today, he realized our dream," said Gary's father, hugging Layla. Layla smiled as Gary's mother and aunt also hugged her.

"Okay, everyone," shouted Jasmine, clapping her hands together. "Look here! Enough of the hugs and kisses. Please don't be so melodramatic, *yaar.* Let's decide the venue of the wedding." She enthusiastically rubbed her palms together in a reflective motion, and she slowly and clearly said, "I am thinking Chittar Palace, Jodhpur. A grand wedding in a royal palace in the Blue City of Jodhpur, set amidst the striking landscape of the Thar Desert. What say you?"

"I absolutely love the palace. I stay there every time I go to Jodhpur for my polo championships. What do you think of it, Mom and Dad?" asked Gary.

"Yes, we love it too. I think it's perfect," said Gary's mother as she looked towards her husband, who was nodding agreeably in consent.

"So it's decided! Let's raise a toast to it and celebrate!" shouted Jasmine gleefully as they raised and tinkled their glasses together in celebration.

The preparations for the wedding began. The palace was booked two weeks later. The Sandhu family made phone calls and sent out invitations to all their friends and relatives. Layla contacted Belinda and told her about the wedding. She sent air tickets for their close hippie friends in Goa to fly to Jodhpur for the wedding. She also phoned her parents in New York and informed them about the wedding, requesting their presence during the ceremony. Layla's parents were overjoyed to hear about the wedding and about the family into which Layla was getting married. They happily and readily gave their consent to attend the wedding.

The wedding shopping began in full swing. Gary's mother bought a beautiful bright red Bridal silk *Lehenga* (a traditional Indian wedding costume for women) for Layla. Gary couldn't take his eyes off Layla when she modelled it, wearing a short-fitted blouse ending below her breasts with a flowing A-line skirt that billowed away from her waist, as well as a veil over her head with its bell-studded ends tinkling and trailing down to the ground. The *lehenga* was bedecked with beads, rhinestones, and *zari* work and had gold embroidery on it. Gary stood agape as he looked at Layla. "You look like a dream," he whispered in her ear. Layla smiled.

Two weeks flew by as they made wedding preparations and bought traditional wedding clothes, glittering gold, and sparkling diamond jewellery. The Sandhu mansion was decorated with lights and marigolds. Relatives and friends started pouring in from all over India and overseas. The days were spent shopping, and in the evenings the house lit up with string and fairy lights hanging from the rooftop and wrapped around plants and bushes. Little lanterns decoratively hung from trees. A canopy of twinkling lights lit up the front entrance from where neighbours and friends, decked in fine clothing and glittery jewellery, would come in for cocktail and dance. They danced all night to the beats of the *dholis*, on the dance floor set up in the front lawn of the house. The party atmosphere intensified with disco lights, and fog engulfing the peppy dancers on the floor. Elderly women stayed indoors to avoid the cold air, and they sang traditional Punjabi wedding folk songs and performed the *Gidda*, a traditional Punjabi dance for women. Outdoors, the *Bhangra* (traditional Punjabi dance) continued all night.

Layla was a good dancer and had no problems swaying to *bhangra* beats with Gary. She also loved snacking on tandoori chicken, chicken tikka, seekh kebobs, and shami kebobs, which were circulated regularly by turbaned waiters in uniforms. Gary made frequent trips to the outdoor bar, set up in a corner of the garden under a tree that was lit up with fairy and lantern lights, to make sure that Layla was getting her drinks on time. Red and white wine, scotch, rum, beer, tequila, martinis, and mojitos flowed freely as the bedecked crowd danced away to *Bhangra* beats under the diamond-studded sky.

The entire Sandhu clan, along with some close friends, boarded the flight to Jodhpur to celebrate the big day. As they walked out of the tiny airport, a fleet of vintage cars awaited their arrival. Layla wiped her eyes and hands with a fragrant, moist face towel that had been dipped in rose water; it was offered to all the guests, presented in silver trays by the turbaned staff dressed in crisp, white coats buttoned to the top. "Welcome to the Sun City," they greeted the guests as they offered the towels. A whiff of warm breeze brushed Layla's face as she put the towel down on the tray. Unlike Chandigarh, Jodhpur did not feel cool to Layla and was quite pleasant in December. *No wonder it's called the Sun City*, thought Layla. The turbaned attendant opened the backseat door of the car, and Layla and Gary slid in.

Layla's blue eyes were wide open as they drove a short distance to Chittar Palace. "Boy, oh boy! This is amazing!" she whispered in wonder at the first sight of the distant, domed structure nestled in the arid desert and surrounded by enchanting sandy slopes, which were covered by shrubs and bushes. As they drove closer, a majestic golden sand stone castle, perched high on a hill, towered above everything else in her view. The sight of it was overwhelmingly beautiful.

"Do you know that this palace is one of my favourite places in the world?" said Gary turning his head towards Layla, who sat huddled close to him and held his arm. "Each time I came to Jodhpur for polo tournaments, I stayed here. Often when I lazed in my balcony, listening to the peacocks calling, I wondered about my queen, whom I would bring here one day. The day is finally here." He smiled looking lovingly towards Layla. She smiled back and then kissed him.

Soon the car drove through the gated driveway and parked in front of the main entrance of the palace. Layla and Gary stepped out as the *darban* (staff attendant) opened the car door for them. A traditional royal welcome awaited them, and they walked arm in arm under a velvet canopy. Trumpets blared, and the drums started beating as they walked up the steps to the central dome. The staff placed garlands of marigolds around their necks and a red dot on their foreheads. A welcome drink of champagne in flutes was presented to all the guests.

Turbaned folk singers seated on a raised platform started singing traditional folk songs as they played on their vast array of instruments. Vibrant female dancers dressed in bright, traditional Rajasthani outfits made of colourful beads and mirror work danced energetically to the music to welcome the guests. The dancers pulled Layla and Gary in for a dance, and the couple danced a minute or two with them before Gary stepped out. He smiled and twinkled at seeing Layla sway and move with full gusto, trying to copy the moves of the dancers. Upon catching Gary's eyes, Layla giggled, stepped out, and hugged Gary. Their families and friends clapped and cheered.

Layla stood still a moment to look at the beautiful, intricately-designed, vaulted central dome of the palace. The entire structure was built with marble and golden yellow sandstone, and it boasted of deft craftsmanship in the Indo-colonial and the art deco style of the 1930s. As the other guests were walked to their respective rooms by the staff, Gary walked Layla out to the lush, sprawling gardens with his arm wrapped around her waist. They held on to their champagne flutes. Tweeting birds, chasing squirrels, and dancing peacocks welcomed them as they sipped on their champagne. A cuckoo cooed in the distance as the orange sun sunk behind an ancient fort on a high hill, lighting up the sky in its crimson radiance and bathing the palace in its golden hue.

"That is where we will be getting married," Gary said, pointing to a magnificent marble gazebo at the centre of the sprawling lawns. Layla turned towards Gary and wrapped her arms around him, and they kissed against the backdrop of the marble gazebo and the ancient castle.

The next afternoon, all of Layla's guests were to arrive, including her friends from Goa and her parents from New York. Gary and Layla awaited every arrival from the airport as they lounged in the lobby area. Suddenly the trumpets blared, and Layla knew they were here. As she edged closer to the main entrance, her eyes welled up at the sight of her parents. Her father and mother stood still with dewy eyes and under a shower of rose petals as they saw their daughter after seven long years.

Layla rushed into their arms as tears rolled down her cheeks. "I am so happy that you came," she managed to whisper between sobbing, sniffing, and crying.

"We are just happy that you look well," whispered her composed, stylish mother. She wore a white knee-length dress accented with pearls and a flamboyant white chapeau with swirling feathers. Gary was the next to greet them, and Layla introduced her parents to him and rest of the Sandhu clan. Greetings and hugs poured in from all directions as the Sandhu family ushered them in, offered refreshments, and led them to their room.

The trumpets blared again, prompting Layla to look towards the entrance. Lo and behold, it was the merry hippie group from Goa! Layla couldn't stop laughing when she saw Belinda, André, Spanish Juan, Handsome Leonardo, Spanish Isabella, Italian Sofia, and American Laura dancing with enthusiastic fervour amongst the traditional dancers. With garlands around their necks and champagne flutes in their raised hands, they whirled and twirled on the black granite floor to the folk music. They whistled and cheered when Gary and Layla joined in with them. "Welcome, lovely friends," greeted Layla and Gary as they hugged and kissed their special guests from Goa.

"Congratulations and celebrations," they sang in a chorus of replies as they danced.

"Holy cow! This palace is so beautiful—right out of a dream!" exclaimed Belinda with a dimpled smile and glitter in her eyes.

"Yes, indeed it is!" said Layla with a wide smile. Then she added, "I am so glad you came, Belinda. I am happy you all are here, and I am excited about everything that life is offering me at the moment. I can't thank the stars enough." She spoke at lightning speed with overwhelming emotion and zesty enthusiasm.

"Aw, I love you, my lovely," said Belinda as she hugged Layla tight.

"Okay, another thing, Belinda. As you know, all this is a family affair—Gary's family, my parents, everyone is here. And you know they all belong to the straight world that is unfamiliar with our ways. Could you please take charge and make sure that everyone maintains a low profile? I mean, have fun, and dance and party, but take care that we don't scandalize any of the families, please."

Belinda broke out in a belly-clenching, roaring fit of laughter. "Of course, my dear! We will make sure there are no scandals," she said, wiping away her tears of laughter. Layla winked and chuckled along.

After a sumptuous meal, family and friends went sightseeing. They visited the mighty Mehrangarh fort. As they reached the very top, Layla and Gary stood amongst cannons on the open porch of the palace, bending over its wall to view the walled and gated old city of Jodhpur, wrapped around the base of the fort with all its cubicle houses painted blue.

"Boy, oh boy! This is so gorgeous! But why are all these houses painted blue?" asked Layla with curiosity.

"Along with being called the Sun City because of its warm weather, Jodhpur is also called the Blue City, because of the colour of its houses. There are many reasons for it. Some say because of the city's sunny weather, and the blue paint deflects heat and keeps the houses cool. Others say the blue colour is associated with the

Brahmins, the priestly class of India, and the families of that caste painted their houses blue. I say it's to keep the mosquitoes at bay." Gary waved a buzzing mosquito away from his face, and Layla laughed.

The guests posed with cannons and weapons and took picture after picture of the Blue City. They then meandered through the winding, looping, colourful medieval streets of old Jodhpur's bazaar, lined by tiny shops on either sides selling bangles, saris, incense, silver and brass artefacts, and temple decorations. Cowbells tinkled on bulls roaming freely by the roadside, a man lazed under a banyan tree, and a group of men played cards under a mango tree. *Tongas*, or small horse carriages, abounded the narrow, crowded bazaar streets as a mode of transportation. A horse neighed in protest as he carried passengers in its buggy.

Gary's mother and Jasmine entered a shop selling *Ghaghara Choli* (traditional women's attire consisting of a short blouse, a long flowing skirt, and a long veil) and ethnic jewellery. They bought traditional clothing and jewellery for all of Layla's female friends from Goa, to wear during the wedding celebrations. They also helped Layla's mother pick up a nice, bright *Ghaghara Choli*.

"Mrs. Smith, this maroon one looks great on you," said Gary's mother as she placed the blouse and veil against Layla's mother's chest.

Jasmine helped Belinda pick her attire "Yes, yes! This orange one for you, *yaar*, definitely," said Jasmine with extreme confidence as she helped the ladies pick up their fancy traditional clothing. "And this red one for you, lady." She continued till all women had bought a couple of pairs each of traditional attire. For the men, Layla's mother had already bought *Sherwanis* (a knee-length coat buttoning to the neck, worn with tight leggings) from Chandigarh.

The turbaned hotel staff that accompanied them in the vintage cars graciously took away their shopping bags and placed them in the luggage compartment of the cars. Everyone was tired of shopping and hungry, so Gary walked all the guests to a small shop that sold lassi, a yogurt drink with which Layla, Belinda, and the hippie group were already familiar. He also ordered some snacks, samosas and kachodis, and everyone devoured them. As they walked out satiated from the tiny shop, beggars scurried in behind them, tugging on to their clothes and motioning to their mouths. "*Paisa,* madam." "I am hungry, sir." Gary took out a wad of hundred-rupee notes and distributed amongst them. Before more would come, they slid inside their cars. The Goa group took a Tonga ride back to the palace hotel.

In the evening, Layla walked over to Belinda and Sophia's room. When she knocked on the door, Sophia let her in. "Okay, girls, get ready in your colourful, fancy outfits. We have a celebration tonight. We are going to dance and party all night long," said Layla, bobbing her shoulders and wiggling her hips as she surveyed the room, looking for her best friend. "Where is Belinda?" she asked curiously.

"In the powder room," Sophia said with a snicker. As Layla barged in the powder room, she saw Belinda crouching over a marble countertop and sniffing in neatly arranged lines of cocaine through a rolled-up bill.

"Hey, Belinda! How did you get this here?" exclaimed Layla in astonishment.

"I sewed a slim packet of cocaine in the hem of my skirt, while travelling on plane from Bombay to Jodhpur. Nobody noticed. Tee-hee!" She giggled mischievously and then added, "But don't you worry, Layla. We will sniff very little. Nobody will know, I promise."

"Well ... okay. As long as you keep your promise, all is fine and dandy with me," said Layla, shrugging her shoulders. After a moment's pause, she added, "Where are André and group? Could you inform them about the party, please?"

"Well, they are on the balcony of their room, lighting up chillums and whispering Bam Bam Bhole. *Whispering,* mind you!" Belinda laughed, throwing her head back.

"Boy, oh boy!" laughed Layla, shaking her head side to side "Well, do let them know to gather in the Palace Banquet Hall at seven sharp, dressed in their best. Okey-dokey?"

"Okey-dokey," agreed Belinda.

At 7:00 p.m., guests gathered in one of the royal banquet halls of the palace, beautifully decorated with marigolds, to celebrate the *mehndi* (henna) and *sangeet* (song and dance) evening. Layla sat on a small, low-legged jute stool placed on a raised platform in one corner of the hall. She wore a green cotton *salwar kameez* with a *phulkari*. A *mehndi* artist sat at her feet and applied the henna paste through a cone, in intricate designs on her hands, arms, and feet. "*Mehndi* is symbolic of love between the bride and the groom," explained the artist as she applied the paste. "I will write Gary's name somewhere hidden in between this design, and you ask your groom to find it, okay?" she said with a twinkling smile. Layla said okay and smiled back. The green *mehndi* felt cool on her palms.

The colourful ladies flocked around other *Mehndi* artists who were applying henna on their palms and feet. Belinda got two peacocks designed on her palms. "Holy cow! I love this!" she exclaimed.

There were professional dance performances followed by *dholis* beating on their *dhols*. Everyone dressed in bright traditional attire and jewellery and danced to the *dhol* beat. Suddenly the drums stopped beating, and everyone heard the thunk of a wooden stick mixed with tinkling bells and a loud female voice, that merrily bellowed, "*Jaago Aaee aa*" (Jaago is coming). She stomped the wooden stick, wrapped in bells on the floor.

Layla was merrily surprised to see one of Gary's aunts standing in the entrance with a steel pot decorated with candles placed on her head. "Jaago means wake up and join in the wedding celebration," she yelled out to explain to those who didn't know. Then she started moving rhythmically, holding the pot with both her hands whilst dancing and singing *Jaago* songs. All the ladies joined in the clapping, singing, and dancing as the pot was passed from head to head of all women.

"Whoa!" exclaimed Belinda as she swirled, whirled, and twirled with the candlelit pot on her head. The rest of their female friends from Goa, along with Layla's mother, especially enjoyed carrying the lit pot on their heads amidst giggles and cheers. The rest of the night was spent singing and dancing. The *dhol* beats continued as women in colourful *Ghagharas* and men in *Sherwanis* with pleated and tailed turbans danced away to glory.

Layla was woken up the next morning at twilight by Gary's mother. All the ladies assembled in the Maharani suite, where Layla was staying. Gary's mother lit four lamps and placed a short-legged jute stool facing them. She asked Layla to sit on the stool so that the glow from the lamps would be reflected on her face. Four women stood on all four sides of Layla, holding on to a thick red rectangular *phulkari* over her head. Gary's mother lovingly applied *Vatna*, a paste made from turmeric powder and mustard oil, on Layla's legs, arms, and face. "This is applied to make the bride appear even more beautiful on her wedding day," she explained as she gently rubbed the paste on Layla's body. All ladies took turns to apply the paste on her.

"I am so loving all of this, Layla," said Belinda as she applied the paste on her legs. "You are no short of a queen these days." She and Layla chuckled.

Layla was then sent to the washroom to take a shower. Once she was out and wrapped in a thick *phulkari*, Layla's dad was called in to slide a set of red and cream ivory bangles (*chura*) on Layla's arms. "This custom is usually done by the bride's maternal uncle, but because he is not here, we thought you might as well do it," said Gary's mother as she explained it to Layla's father.

"Of course, of course! With pleasure, Mrs. Sandhu," he exclaimed agreeably as he slid the bangles over Layla's wrists. Jasmine then handed *kaliras* (gold-plated, hanging traditional ornaments) to Layla's father, who tied these to the ivory bangles. Layla loved the tinkling sound the *kaliras* made as she held them next to her ear and shook them merrily. Layla was then left alone with the make-up artist in the room who would help her dress for the wedding.

After going through the *Vatna* ceremony, Gary stepped out of the shower wearing his gold-embroidered *Sherwani* and a red turban. He had grown stubble in the past 10 days, as all clean-shaven Sikh grooms did, in anticipation of his wedding day when he would have to wear a turban. Jasmine lovingly tied the *Sehra*, a head dress with garlands that dangle over the groom's face, around his turban. Gary was then handed the *kirpan*, a decorated sword that he wore on a belt to the side of his waist. All dressed and ready for the big day, Gurveer Singh Sandhu looked like an Indian maharaja in his *Sehra*, *Sherwani*, and *Kirpan*.

The entire Sandhu family circled around Gary as he mounted the decorated horse amidst cheers and clapping. His sister-in-law marked his eyes with kohl as he sat on the horse. "This is to ward off any evil eye, away from this handsome groom," she said with a giggle. Gary's nephew became his *sarbala* (the best man), who also mounted the horse while wearing the same clothes as Gary.

The *baraat* was a royal procession. A 20-piece band led the way, blowing trumpets and beating drums. Gary followed the band mounted on a horse and surrounded by sentries and *dholis*. Jasmine and the rest of Gary's cousins danced joyously in front of the band. Layla, her parents, and her friends from Goa awaited the arrival of the *baraat* (wedding procession) in the central dome of the palace, dressed in brightly-coloured traditional attire, the women in *lehengas* and the men in *Sherwanis*. Layla stood in one corner holding a *varmala* (a heavy garland made of Jasmine and roses) in her densely-bangled, *kalira*-decorated, and *mehndi*-adorned hands. She looked like a queen in her heavily-beaded and gold-embroidered red silk *lehenga Choli,* and her tinkling and trailing rhinestone-studded veil. She wore a big red dot between and small red and white dots over her fine eyebrows. Diamond-studded gold bangles glittered on her wrists, and a long heavy necklace (*Rani Haar*) made of uncut diamonds and stunning emeralds rested on her bosom, hanging down to her navel. Diamond- and emerald-studded long earrings (*jhumkas*) hung from her ears, a round diamond-studded gold pendant (*tikka*) hung over her forehead, and an oval emerald-studded gold pendant hung on the left side of her head (*paasa*). Diamond rings shimmered on her toes, and bell-studded anklets tinkled around her ankles. Rhinestones glittered all over her attire, shining from a distance. Layla was shining in diamonds from head to toe.

Drums started beating, and trumpets blared at the arrival of the *baarat*. Gary dismounted the horse. Under a velvet canopy, he walked up the steps leading to the central dome, with his family following behind him. Under a shower of rose petals, Gary and the Sandhu family entered the dome. A *varmala* was handed to Gary, and he held it in his slightly raised hands as he walked towards the flowered pedestal set up at a central spot. His family stood in a circle inside the dome and on the balconies above. Nine holy men in three rows started blowing conch shells to announce the arrival of the bride, along with her father by leading the way as Layla, held by her father, slowly walked towards the pedestal behind the priests holding a *varmala*. As Layla and Gary stepped on the pedestal, standing face to face, they lovingly looked at one another and then exchanged garlands with twinkling eyes and wide smiles. Trumpets blared again as the guests showered rose petals from the balconies above.

Gary was able to steal a moment alone with Layla after the *Varmala*. "Today, you look like an *apsara,*" he whispered in her ear.

"What is an *apsara?*" asked Layla.

"A beautiful celestial maiden, not of this earth but of heaven, dancing somewhere in the clouds above," he murmured while caressing her cheek, "Layla, the *apsara*, dancing in the sky with diamonds." They hugged.

Guests walked outside to a part of the sprawling gardens covered on all four sides with bright pink bougainvillea. The sun was partly covered by grey clouds, and a pleasant breeze blew over the flowers and trees as the guests enjoyed their lavish breakfast, arranged in over 50 decorative satin-lined stalls, from Continental to South Indian, Punjabi, Gujarati, and Rajasthani. Tree leaves rustled in the wind, and birds chirped around bushes as the guests ate, smiled, laughed, and mingled.

After breakfast, the guests were ushered to the central lawns for *Anand Karaj* (the Sikh marriage ceremony). The *pheras* (nuptial rounds) were to be held at the raised marble pagoda situated at the centre of the lush green lawns. The Sri Guru Granth Sahib (holy book of the Sikhs) was placed in the centre of the pagoda, on a raised platform, the *beed*. A shiny red cloth was tied above the holy book by tying its four ends to the four pillars of the pagoda. A Sikh holy priest sat behind the *beed*, swaying a long horse-hair brush over the holy book as he recited hymns. The guests were seated cross-legged on white sheets spread on the lawns, below the white marble pagoda. Gary was seated on the pagoda, on the right-hand side, facing the holy book. Layla's father, wearing a *Sherwani* and a turban, walked Layla towards the pagoda, holding her gently by her shoulder.

Belinda, Sophia, Isabella, Laura, and a few more of Layla's female friends from Goa walked as bridesmaids behind Layla, holding flowers. Layla's face was covered in a netted veil as she was walked up the white marble stairs of the pagoda and was seated on the left side of Gary by her father. Layla's father, as prompted by Gary's father, placed the end of Gary's stole in Layla's hand. As the priest sung hymns, Gary and Layla stood up. Gary started walking in front as Layla walked slowly behind him, holding his stole. Gary and Layla took three nuptial rounds around the holy book, seating themselves after every round. As they stood up to take the fourth and final nuptial round, the guests started showering rose petals on them. They continued till the couple completed the final round, bowed down in front of the holy book, and seated themselves. Now they were officially Mrs. and Mr. Sandhu.

After the wedding ceremony, the bar was thrown open, and guests enjoyed cocktail and snacks as an American band entertained them with jazz music. The dance floor filled up with couples, swaying slowly in each other's arms to smooth soul, jazz, and blues. As the afternoon progressed and the sun peeked out of the clouds, the music picked up pace, and guests jigged away on the floor, shaking a leg to the rock and roll, samba, and rumba, along with the international dancers who performed on the decorated stage in front of dance floor. After a lavish lunch, everyone retired to their rooms to rest and get ready for the evening party.

A full moon hung low over the lush garden, decorated in string and fairy lights, wrapped around every tree, shrub, and plant. White satin bowed chairs were arranged in circles around satin-clothed tables, lit with candles in the centre that were arranged in three-piece silver candle holders. For this special evening, Gary donned a black-and-white, velvet-lined tuxedo. Layla wore a white halter gown decorated with lace, sequins, and tiny pearls. Diamonds around Layla's neck and fingers shimmered as the couple made a grand entry arm in arm, walking down the red carpeted stairs with Layla's long dress trailing behind her. Drums rolled and trumpets blared at their arrival. Colourful fireworks lit up the sky as Layla and Gary cut the cake. Gary then led Layla to the dance floor for their first dance as husband and wife. Couples joined in under the star-speckled sky. The palace and its people shimmered in the glow of the full moon as the newlywed couple and their friends and family danced the night away.

Chapter 12

I'm Going Away

Love me two times, baby,
Love me twice today.
Love me two times, girl,
I'm goin' away.

—Jim Morrison

Back in Goa, life was beautiful. Sun-filled, long, and lazy days were spent lounging around on the warm, sunny, salty, sandy beach. People sang, danced, laughed, played, smoked, and sniffed by the ocean under the swaying coconut palm trees. Layla and Gary were living a happy life as husband and wife. The two lived in Gary's compact house, inside a private part of his hotel. He mostly dropped off Layla at Anjuna beach in the mornings, and he stayed busy with work all day. Layla hung around with Belinda, André, and the rest of her hippie friends.

Whenever Gary could find time off work, he would spend it at the beach with Layla and the rest of her friends. He drank his beer while the others smoked chillums, sniffed lines, or dropped acid. He would watch Layla admirably as she smoked grass through her stylish bong, seated comfortably against a satin cushion in one corner of the room full of her smoking and sniffing friends. Her eyelids would shut lightly over her deep blue sleepy eyes, and her pretty, dry mouth would open up partly in a pout of bliss. He loved everything about her, even her pot-smoking habit. What he loved more about her was that marijuana was her one and only drug of choice. She did not experiment with any of the hard drugs like cocaine or smack; they did not agree with her, she had told Gary. Gary was also aware of the fact that she was a responsible smoker. She knew her limits and almost never lost her composure. That was what made Layla special, and that was why he loved her. Gary simply wanted to see Layla smile, and smile she did in his loving arms.

Gary wanted to give Layla her much-dreamed-of life, so he decided to build their holiday home on the beaches of Anjuna. He bought a large, dilapidated house from a local Goan, got it razed to the ground, and then asked Layla to design her dream home any way she liked. "I want to build a beautiful Spanish beach villa over-laden with flowers, with arched doorways and large windows to let in the Goan sun," she stated with raised arms, palms facing the sun, closed eyes, and a blissful smile. She stood at the site of her would-be home, bathing in the sunlight with Gary, Belinda, and the architect. From that day onwards, Layla was busy dreaming of and designing her new home, working closely with the architect who tried to give shape to her every whim and fancy.

When she was not designing, she made a couple of short trips with Belinda to Kashmir and Nepal, to collect art pieces and artefacts for her new home. During these trips, she noticed Belinda. Layla felt guilty about being a bit too preoccupied with her own life to notice what was going on with her dear friend. Belinda had lost a lot of weight and was now reed thin. She was neither sleeping enough nor eating enough, and she was sniffing line after line of cocaine. She stayed buzzed and wired at all times, like a zombie. In order to get some sleep, she would pop a few pills of Valium in her mouth every night.

One morning in Kathmandu, while Belinda was fiddling around with her fork at the breakfast table of the Royal Hotel, Layla placed her hand over Belinda's, leaned over, and said with a downcast glance, "Belinda, dear, I am sorry that I have been busy with my new life with Gary lately." She paused, looked up, and then added, "I see that you are not doing well at all. You are walking down a path of destruction. It is not fun and games. We did not come to Goa for this. Anything can happen to you at any time, if you continue at this pace. Please, Belinda, look after yourself—and cut down on your cocaine consumption. Please."

Belinda looked up at Layla with her bloodshot eyes and enlarged pupils. She rubbed Layla's shoulder and said with feigned cheer, "Hey! Don't worry. Nothing is bad at all. You are taking it all way too seriously. I agree, though, that I need to cut down on my coke consumption. And I will, soon enough. For now, just relax and stop worrying! Okay, Love?"

"Okey-dokey!" answered Layla after a moment's silence. Then she added, "As long as you keep your promise and try hard to give it up. Okay?"

Once back in Goa, Layla ran into André on the beach. While standing under a coconut tree, she talked to him about Belinda. André seemed to have given up all hope, and he shook his head dismissively before saying, "I can't see Belinda go down that route." Then he placed his hands upon his hips and said, "She is lost in a vicious circle. I've lost far too many close friends in this circle, and they could never make it out. I have tried my very best with Belinda, but nothing seems to work. I have to stay a bit distant and detach myself from her, if I want to maintain my peace of mind and sanity." André had a helpless look on his face.

Layla couldn't blame him. She dejectedly walked away after squeezing his shoulder and saying, "I understand."

Belinda would get angry when André wouldn't see her for days in a row, or when he wouldn't answer his door. "He doesn't love me anymore!" she had cried on Layla's shoulder many times.

It was March 1976, and Layla was two months into worrying about Belinda and designing her new home. Summer was fast approaching, and the hippies of Goa were making preparations to leave for the west in the next month or two. Hardly any hippies or Westerners stayed in Anjuna during the hot monsoon months, when it rained incessantly. The ones who could be seen idling around at that time would either be the local Goans or hippies who had fallen on hard times. Others made money in the West during summer so they could support themselves and party in Goa from October to March. Drug smuggling was one of their preferred, quick ways of making money. They'd pack a lump of hash in their bags and sell it overseas. Those working at a higher level, with strong connections, smuggled heroin into India from Afghanistan and Pakistan, and in turn they smuggled it into the West and made huge profits. Handsome Leonardo was one of them.

One evening while Layla was visiting Belinda, friends gathered at Belinda's house. Spanish Juan, Italian Sophia, Spanish Isabella, Handsome Leonardo, and a few others sat around her Afghani rug, sniffing and snorting while Pink Floyd music played in the background. A tall, lean English man wearing Buddha pants and a blue satin vest with silver stars sat in the middle of the rug, dispensing cocaine and smack. Long golden locks fell over his dainty face as he bent over to make lines of cocaine on a gilded mirror.

"Who is he?" whispered Layla in Belinda's ear.

"British Alex. Isn't he cute?" Belinda said with a grin. "I find him very sweet, and he always carries huge amounts of cocaine and smack on him, which he sells on the beach. But to me, he gives it for free." She chuckled.

"Your Highness! Could you please move forward?" he called out, motioning to Belinda in his accented king's English. He placed a nugget of smack on aluminium foil that he held from one end, and Belinda held it from the other. Then he held a lit candle underneath the foil. Belinda inhaled the smack smoke through a rolled-up note and sat back in bliss. Layla watched Belinda and Alex closely as she smoked her bong. Now she knew from where Belinda had been getting her free supply of cocaine and smack.

"Has anybody seen Spanish Juan?" asked Sophia, who was looking for him all over the house. "Juan, where are you? Hello?" She walked from room to room, searching for him. Spanish Juan, who had been sitting in one corner, was completely consumed with the process of injecting powdered cocaine mixed with water into his arm, and he was now nowhere to be seen. "Juan has my packet of cocaine with him. Where has this man gone? He has been doing too much coke and has now completely lost his marbles," Sophia complained as she stomped her feet in frustration. Everyone started looking for Spanish Juan.

Belinda walked inside her bedroom on the top floor. The room was in shambles, and things lay scattered around. All her clothes were thrown in a heap on the ground. Her bedsheets were tangled, and a broken glass littered her bed. The flower vase was knocked over and broken. Belinda walked over to the attached store room and found it locked. She called out, "Juan! Juan, open the door!" No one answered. "He must be in here. Come here, guys," shouted Belinda as she pushed hard on the door. Everyone gathered around the door, and they banged, pushed, and pounded on the door.

"Juan, open the door!" shouted Leonardo as he pushed and kicked. "Open!" he yelled again. No answer. Finally, with one hard push of his shoulder, he broke open the door that slammed against the wall.

Spanish Juan was frightened and huddled in one corner, and with his one hand he pressed his knees tightly against his chest. With his other hand, he flashed a torch at the onlookers. His hair was in disarray, and his red freckles were shining bright in the glow of the flashlight. "Stay away! All of you, stay away!" he yelled with a terrified look on his face. "Don't come near me! You can't catch me!" he yelled.

"Juan, stand up! You need to go home and get some sleep," said Leonardo cautiously as he inched towards Juan.

"No! Don't, don't!" shouted Juan as he briskly slid open the window behind him, and at full tilt he climbed over and jumped on the roof. Leonardo leaped on him and caught his dangling foot.

"No! Let him go, or he will fall down from the roof," shouted Alex. Leonardo let go. By the time everyone ran downstairs and outdoors, Juan was completely out of sight.

Everyone held flashlights and dispersed in different directions, shouting. "Juan! Juan, where are you? They searched all over the beach, through the ravines, around the paddy fields, and in and around the houses of friends, but Spanish Juan couldn't be found. After searching for nearly four hours, they finally gave up and returned to Belinda's house.

They resumed their sniffing and snorting. "Juan has lost his mind. Cocaine binging, no food, and no sleep for days on end, and this is what happens: cocaine-induced paranoia," stated Italian Sophia in despair. "Now each time he injects excessive cocaine, he loses his mind and starts freaking out."

"Yes, I remember, he did the same thing at my residence last time," said Alex in his British accent. "He injected too much cocaine, turned lunatic, completely destroyed my domicile, and then sprinted away. The next morning, we found him asleep at his abode." He shrugged. "It's frightening, though—very frightening!"

The group sat around till the wee hours of the morning, talking, sniffing, worrying, and dozing. At twilight, Sophia decided to take a dip in the ocean while others still lazed around the Persian rug in Belinda's house. "Aaah!" They heard Sophia's loud shriek and ran out. They found Spanish Juan's body washed ashore at the beach.

Everyone stood still, shocked and stunned. Layla collapsed. The police was informed and so was Gary. The police was taking away Spanish Juan's body for post-mortem, when Gary approached Belinda's house. Layla had by then regained consciousness. She lay on the mattress, sobbing and sulking as others sat around her with mournful faces and heavy hearts. Layla broke down in a fit of tears as she saw Gary walk in. Gary hugged her and caressed her back .She fainted again. Gary picked her up and drove her straight to the doctor in the nearest town. The doctor examined Layla and then announced "Congratulations! She is pregnant." Layla hugged Gary and cried tears of joy and sorrow.

After a few days of sadness and mourning, life continued at Anjuna. Layla was neither drinking alcohol nor smoking bongs due to her pregnancy. She spent most of her time surveying the construction of her Spanish villa. When she was not at the construction site, she was either painting or singing and playing guitar by the beach. She painted the sea, the sunrise, and the sunset. She painted a portrait of Gary standing next to his horse Top Gun. She painted Belinda with closed eyes and flying hair, lost in a trance amongst the stars. She painted Spanish Juan swimming in the sea on a full moon night. *Juan!* A strange sort of sadness had crept inside the warm, salty Anjuna beach air, or maybe it was just the fast-approaching summer. People had started parting with their luggage and backpacks. Day by day, the beach was become more bare and desolate.

André left for France. Belinda decided to spend the summer in Nepal with Alex. Layla stayed busy with her house construction and her travels with Gary. The two had postponed their honeymoon for the summer. Now, they celebrated their month-long honeymoon travelling across Europe, sipping coffee in the cafés of Paris, cruising through the canals of Venice and Amsterdam, and meandering through the white-washed houses of the Greek islands. Once back, they visited Chandigarh a couple of times to meet family, who were overjoyed and anxiously awaiting the arrival of the precious bundle of joy, due to be born in December.

Time flew by, and before they knew, October had rolled in, and the beach started filling up. Belinda and Alex were back from Nepal. Belinda was even thinner than before. She had dark circles and bags under her eyes, and bones poked out of her thin skin. Her hand trembled as it held a rolled-up note to sniff the powder. Her nose bled often from the dryness caused by sniffing cocaine, so she carried a little bottle of vitamin E oil with her at all times, which she applied to her nostrils. Layla had worried about Belinda all summer long, and she had watched her house being built while caressing her belly. Layla was now seven months pregnant, and the Spanish villa was up and ready to move into.

Nestled amongst tall palms, the house had a white stucco exterior and a red clay tile roof. Wrought-iron details accented the exterior. The entry walkway had an arched gate in the front, with decorative lanterns hanging on either side of it. The path was lined by blooming flowers, and it led to a heavily carved wooden front door. Solar lamp posts decorated each side of the walkway and the courtyard. A wooden fence covered in ivy surrounded the yard. Flowers bloomed in baskets attached to the exterior of the arched windows of the house. Gary had built a house for Layla that was straight out of a fairy tale.

Inside the house, a mix of the granite, marble, and decorative tile floors gleamed and felt cool on Layla's bare feet. Layla got the walls painted an earthen yellow and decorated them with Tibetan and Nepalese paintings, decorative mirrors, Afghani wall hangings, and Kashmiri tapestries. Persian rugs covered a part of the tiled floor in every room. Earthen ware, chimes, singing bowls, Buddha statues, silver and brass artefacts, and decorative bongs adorned the brightly lit house. Sunlight bathed every room through its large bay windows during the day, and at night flames flickered in decorative wall candle holders and lanterns, lighting up the house in a warm orange glow. This was the perfect life of Layla and Gary.

Layla and Gary threw a house-warming party. The house was lit up with string lights hanging from the roof and fairy lights wrapped around the palm trees. All their friends dressed in glitter and shimmer, and they jived to the tunes of the live band. Uniformed waiters from Gary's hotel catered to the guests, serving them wine and snacks. André and his group lit chillums in the back yard, yelling "Bam Bhole" and "Bam Shankar." Belinda and Alex offered lines of cocaine to guests gathered around the Persian rug. Layla mingled with a glass of orange juice in her hand, and Gary had a pint of beer. Guests danced, stomped, and sang all night under the stars. Around twilight, a few people started leaving for their homes, a few lazed around the Afghani rug, some dozed off, and others still sniffed and snorted.

Belinda sat cross-legged on the Persian rug, beating African drums beside Alex, who sat with his back against the closed door of an attached bedroom. Buzzed, wired, and edgy, Belinda shook her head and bangs from side to side as she beat the drums harder and harder. Suddenly Alex jumped up, feeling something moist seep through his Buddha pants. "Yikes! It's blood" he shrieked as he glanced at his palm after rubbing it against his pants. "And it's coming through the slit under the closed door that I was leaning against." His eyes followed the trail of blood. Everyone gathered around him as he pushed on the door, which hit a body lying against it in a pool of blood. It was Italian Sophia, who had bled a little from her nose and mouth—and profusely from her belly. The sharp, broken glass of a tripped-over vase was still stuck inside her stomach. They called the police and the doctor, who declared her dead. The possible cause was a drug overdose that caused a seizure. During her seizure, she probably tipped over the vase and fell over it. The police sealed the site and took the body away for post-mortem.

Gloom had seeped in the walls of Layla's dream home and the sands of Anjuna beach. Gary worried about Layla. He got the house cleaned thoroughly and sprinkled holy water in it. He invited Sikh priests to bring in the holy book and continuously chant prayers inside the house for three days in a row (*Akhand Paath*). The holy book was placed, and prayers were recited in the room where Sophia had died. After purification of the house, Gary decided to take a little break from Anjuna beach.

The two decided to spend a few days in Chandigarh. They flew to Delhi and then drove to Chandigarh. The family was very excited to see them.

The next day, at 5:30 a.m., there was a knock on the door. "*Beta ji*, wake up. We are all going for a jog by the lake," called Gary's father. They changed into their track suits, opened the gate, and got ready to jog to the lake, which was hardly a 10-minute walk. The sun was rising in the east, and all was aglow in its soft orange hue. Mrs. Sharma, their next-door neighbour, stood on the roof of her house, facing the sun. With raised arms, she held a tilted copper vessel high above her head and was seemingly pouring the water to the sun that flowed down on the ground.

"She is doing *Surya Namaskar*, a salutation to the rising sun" explained Gary to Layla, who was watching her curiously. Mrs. Sharma waved at the Sandhu family with a wide smile after she had done her prayers with folded hands, bowing down to the sun. The Sandhu family waved back with wide smiles.

As they jogged to the lake, Layla noticed the clean, wide, almost bare roads of Chandigarh. The roads met at right angles and had large roundabouts at intersections. Birds chirped around bright orange flowers of *Gulmohar* trees that formed a canopy over the side road on which they jogged. Crows cawed, and uniformed school children giggled as they rode the rickshaw on their way to school. Auto rickshaw drivers enjoyed their steaming cups of morning tea as they discussed the newspaper headlines, awaiting early morning passengers.

Swans and ducks swam over the lake as the Sandhu family jogged by. Gary's father, who was jogging by Layla's side, stole the chance to talk about Chandigarh with pride. "This city is by far the most well-planned city of India. The master plan of the city was prepared by the French architect Le Corbusier, who neatly planned and divided it into sectors." He paused to sip on a bottle of water and then continued. "You must go with Gary to see the largest of Le

Corbusier's, the Open Hand structure, or *la Main Ouverte*, as it is called in French. It stands 26 metres high. According to Corbusier, the hand stands for peace and reconciliation," Gary's father continued the monologue throughout the jog, and Layla continued nodding in agreement. "You see this tower here, inside the lake? It was basically constructed to measure the water level, but people have been jumping from it to commit suicide. It is now called the Suicide Point." Layla made a sad face in response as she jogged. "And you see those hills behind the lake? Those are the Himalayan foothills. You must go there with Gary. Gary went to school in those hills ..."

The Sandhu family jogged back home. After showering, they had spicy *Alloo ka Parathas* (potato-stuffed flatbread) for breakfast. "These are yummy, Bali ram ji. Very good! Thank you!" said Layla to the family cook as she licked her fingers while seated around the large dining table. Gary had planned the day. They were going to Sector 17, the city centre, to watch the Hindi movie *Charas* in Neelam Cinema Hall.

"*Charas*? Are you serious? Ha!" Layla threw back her head and laughed. "So we are going to watch the movie *Hash*. Couldn't you find one with a better title, Gary?" She continued laughing as Gary chuckled.

Gary, Layla, and the family stood outside a single-screen cinema hall that had a huge, hand-painted movie poster of the movie *Charas* hanging outside it. Sohan Singh was sent to line up in the long queue to buy tickets. Suddenly, the lined crowd dispersed with sad faces. The ticket counter had been shut down, and a "House Full" sign hung over it. Still, Sohan Singh walked towards the family with an ear-to-ear grin. He had managed to buy the tickets in black. Gary explained to Layla that *black* meant paying almost double the price for those tickets. Many small-time conmen and shifty characters had a made a business of it. They bought the tickets cheap but would sell them at double the price to those in need, and they made a juicy profit in this little scam. Gary chuckled as he explained, and Layla giggled.

Once inside the dark theatre, they showed their tickets to a man with a flashlight, who was seating everyone. He first flashed the light on their tickets and then flashed it in on their row. They followed the flash, tracked their row, and then sat down on the foam-filled, worn-out red seats. Layla's seat was ripped open, and its foam and metal spring lay bare through the tear. Gary exchanged his seat with Layla's. "I don't mind it," he said with a smile. As the movie played, Gary kept whispering the story in Layla's ear. During the interval, Gary bought popcorn and Coca-Cola for the entire family. Layla enjoyed watching the lead actor and actress of the movie singing songs in the streets of Rome as she popped popcorn in her mouth. "You see this guy, the hero of the movie?" said Gary in a whisper.

"Yes! What about him?" whispered back Layla.

"His name is Dharmendra, and he is Dad's distant cousin," informed Gary.

"Really? That's great! He is so handsome," whispered Layla with twinkling eyes.

"Though he is already married, there are rumours that he is in a serious relationship with this leading actress, Hema Malini."

"Hmm. Interesting!" murmured Layla as she popped popcorn in her mouth.

After the movie was over, they walked over to the Indian Coffee House for a late lunch. "This place is very special for us, Layla," said Gary's mother with a twinkle. "Papa and I have been coming here regularly for our special Sunday dates." Her green eyes shined bright, and her diamond nose pin glittered in her Roman nose as she giggled.

"Yes! Our special romantic dates." Gary's father smiled as the two exchanged romantic glances. Layla and Gary smiled along with them.

"How cute!" said Layla.

They had *dosas* in the coffee house. Apparently, that was what it was famous for.

They shopped around Sector 17, and Gary's mother helped Layla pick up a few saris and a few sets of *Salwar Kameez*. Layla modelled, placing the shirts against her chest and wrapping the stoles around her neck. "I especially love this white and golden one on you, Layla. You look beautiful in it!" commented Gary. Layla smiled and bought half a dozen sets of *Salwar Kameez* and a couple of saris. She gleefully returned home with bags full of clothing.

Once home, they showered and changed into their night suits. It was Friday, and at 8:00 p.m. sharp, Doordarshan, the one and only government-owned national channel, telecasted *Chitrahaar*, a 30-minute Indian cinema songs program that Gary's mother, along with the house staff, watched religiously. For half an hour everyone gathered in the room and stayed glued to the television set. Layla, Gary, and his parents tinkled their glasses as they sipped on their drinks and watched Indian actors singing and dancing. After dinner, the family went for a 30-minute stroll outside the house. Once back, they watched the English News Bulletin, and then they retired to bed.

The next morning, Layla and Gary got ready to drive up the hills. "The best thing I love about Chandigarh is that it takes only 30 minutes to drive up the lush, green, beautiful Himalayan foothills," said Gary to Layla as he sat around the mahogany dining table and devoured his stuffed *Paratha* with yogurt. "I also can't wait to show you my boarding school," he added like an excited little boy.

"I can't wait to see it either," Layla replied.

After breakfast, Layla and Gary hugged his parents, who blessed them. Gary dashed towards the Black Jag and slid into the driver's seat while Layla sat beside him. "Are you not taking Sohan Singh to drive you both?" asked Gary's mother with strained eyebrows.

"No, Mom. Not on this romantic drive," he chuckled.

"Okay, then. Drive carefully. Have fun!" said Gary's mother.

"Enjoy yourselves!" said Gary's father as the two waved goodbye.

After another 20 minutes of driving on the plains, suddenly the road started winding up the green hills. Misty air surrounded them and the mountains as the two drove up. "The Himalayas are called the land of the *Devas*. Many ancient seers and yogis have meditated in these hills. That's why you feel this bliss," said Gary as he glanced at Layla. "People say that there are still some immortal yogis who are even today meditating in the Himalayan caves. Many Hindu deities are said to have their abodes in the Himalayas."

"How interesting," murmured Layla, enraptured by the beauty surrounding her.

"We are going to *Kasauli*, a small town and cantonment established by the British raj in 1842, when they ruled over India. It was established as a colonial hill station, to escape the summer heat," explained Gary with his eyes on the road. He paused and then added, "That's where my school is also located." The drive was getting more pleasant and picturesque as they drove up higher. Tall, dense pines swayed in a gentle breeze as birds chirped and monkeys frolicked from tree to tree. Tiny shops selling pickles, juices, and beer lined the winding road.

Gary parked his car by the roadside and walked over to a pickle shop to get his mother's favourite pickles packed for her. Layla opened the car door and stepped out for a moment to breathe in the fresh mountain air. She was peeling a banana to snack on it when suddenly a little monkey pounced on her hand in an attempt to grab the banana. Layla shrieked, threw the banana, hopped on the car seat, and slammed the door. She then cracked opened the window and placed a pack of bananas by the roadside for the monkeys to enjoy. She smiled as she watched a monkey pounce on it and carry it away in a jiffy.

Soon the two entered the tiny town of Kasauli, nestled amongst dense pine trees. Gary parked the car, and the two walked down the cobbled streets of the old town, enjoying the flower-laden lawns in front of the colonial-style bungalows, the old churches, and the clock tower. As they strolled, they felt and heard the musical *pitter-patter* of tiny raindrops falling on the tree leaves and then dribbling down on them. Layla leisurely swirled and twirled like a feather in a gentle breeze with arms wide open, she closed her eyes and faced skywards as the tiny drops fell on her face. Gary gave a wide smile of joy.

The two sprinted back to the car and slid in it as the rain started falling in torrents. Gary drove through the narrow, meandering roads shrouded by pine and deodar trees as heavy sheets of rain lashed against the car's windows.

Suddenly he parked in front of a large, colonial-style building. "That's my school, St. Lawrence." Gary pointed while seated inside the car. "I studied here and lived in it for 10 years." After a moment's pause, he added, "Because Dad was serving in the Indian Army, he would keep getting posted and relocated from one station to another. In order to provide me with a stable education, they sent me to this boarding school. I cried here, I laughed here, I've had good and bad days here." Gary looked intensely in Layla's eyes and smiled. "You are so precious to me, Layla, that I feel like sharing everything with you," he whispered while stroking Layla's cheek. "Every place I have ever visited, anything and everything that's special and close to my heart—I want to show you everything, my love." Layla looked back in his eyes with deep, overwhelming love as he rubbed his fingers against her mouth and cheeks. After a moment of silence, they kissed passionately.

Layla then whispered, "Same here, Gary. I want to share everything with you too. I want to show you my school in New York, and the penthouse that I grew up in, over my father's lavish hotel on Fifth Avenue, and the nightclubs Belinda and I sneaked into with fake

IDs." She giggled. "I want to show you the Haight Ashbury district of San Francisco, where I lived for a few years. I want you to meet my nanny in New York, who literally brought me up. I want you to meet all my family, near and distant, just the way I met yours."

"Yes, Layla. Yes! Soon enough we will plan a trip to meet everyone and see everything that belongs to you." They kissed again amidst a show of lightning and thunder. Gary started the car. "Now, let's get out of here and head back before we get caught in this heavy storm."

"Sure! But I want to sit on the back seat because I am feeling nauseous in the front," said Layla.

"Sure, go ahead," said Gary as Layla opened the car door and hopped on the back seat. Gary turned on the headlights, and dark grey clouds completely shrouded the setting sun, creating a sombre, grey tone.

Gary slowly and carefully drove through the winding roads that circled tall mountains. He furrowed his eyebrows as he tried to concentrate on the dark, windy road ahead. Hard sheets of furious rain hit ruthlessly against the car windows. Loud thunder repeatedly followed the flashes of lightning. Tree leaves trembled in the howling winds.

Suddenly, Gary shouted and braked hard to avoid hitting an old woman walking in front of him. She had suddenly appeared after a sharp mountainous turn. Layla shrieked, and within a flash, the car spun out of control and slid down a dark ditch.

Chapter 13

Our Love Becomes a Funeral Pyre

The time to hesitate is through,
No time to wallow in the mire.
Try now, we can only lose,
And our love becomes a funeral pyre.
Come on baby, light my fire.

—*Jim Morrison*

When Layla opened her eyes, she was in a hospital. Through her blurry vision, she saw a figure standing beside her. "Gary! Gary, is that you?" She groped at the hazy form.

The figure clenched Layla's hands and broke down in a fit of tears. The face, eyes, and hands started becoming distinct. It was Gary's mother. "Are you okay, Layla?" she managed to ask between her sobs and sniffles.

"Where is Gary?" asked Layla in a frightened voice. Gary's mother's throat closed, and she could not answer. Layla jolted her in anger. "Where is Gary? Answer me!" she shouted.

"He is no more, Layla," uttered Gary's mother with a blank gaze as tears trickled down her cheeks.

Layla sat still. No thought, no feeling, no emotion—her mind was silent. She could clearly hear the footsteps of the nurses scurrying by. The ceiling fan whooshed above her head, stirring the warm air. A wall clock beside her bed was ticking away the hands of time. Layla felt herself breathing in and breathing out.

"Layla, are you okay? Are you okay?" whimpered Gary's mother as she shook her by the shoulders. Layla gazed blankly at the emptiness that surrounded her. The emptiness stared back at her. Gary's mother gently wrapped her arms around Layla and said, "It is *Waheruru's* (God's) will, his *Hukum* (order), and we have to abide by it. By his grace, you and the little life inside you are fine. It is nothing less than a miracle." She kissed Layla's head and caressed her as tears continued to stream down her cheeks. Suddenly, all turned dark around Layla, and she fainted in Gary's mother's tender arms.

When Layla opened her eyes next, she sat up and looked around her hospital bed. Gary's mother, father, Jasmine, Bhuaji—everyone stood around her. A lump formed in Layla's throat, and her eyes welled up. A lone tear rested at the edge of her right eye, and then it trickled down. She cried! The family comforted her with heavy hearts and dewy eyes.

That fateful night, when their car had fallen down the ditch, Gary had died on the spot due to a critical head injury, even though the ditch was not very deep. Layla received minor injuries, and miraculously the baby inside her stomach remained unscathed. A passer-by had informed the police, and the two were taken to the hospital while Layla was unconscious. The search of the car revealed the information of the injured. The parents were informed, and Gary was declared dead on arrival. The family was devastated. Layla had regained consciousness after two days. The doctors now deemed her fit to go home.

All seemed dismal and bleak. In a flash, Layla's world had turned upside down. Till yesterday, her life had seemed like a dream too beautiful to be true. Today, it was a nightmare that Layla did not want to go through. She had suicidal thoughts, but Gary's family surrounded her at all times and made sure that she was fine. She stared into emptiness while she lay on a bed that was covered with red roses just a year ago.

The Sandhu family's friends and relatives started pouring in from cities, villages, and overseas. All of the living room's furniture was stacked in one room, and its Persian carpet was covered with crisp white sheets. On these sheets sat the Sandhu family's friends, and relatives. Most of them quietly wept, sniffled, and sobbed. A noisy few whined, cried, bawled, and howled. Ladies from villages, with veil-covered faces, wailed and beat their chests as they sang Gary's praise.

White tents and white sheets covered the sprawling lawns of the Sandhu mansion. Over 500 people dressed in white, gathered to bid final farewell to Gary on the day of the cremation. Gary's body was brought home from the hospital and was given a yogurt bath by a few male members of the family. They dressed the body in fine clothes, placed it on a hearse, and then displayed it for viewing by placing the hearse on the floor of the living room. The body was covered in white sheet, with colourful flowers and garlands placed all around it. Incense burnt by the side of the corpse. Gary's mother sat beside the body and recited the Sikh prayers while the guests paid homage, placing flowers and saying small prayers as they bowed and passed by. Layla sat in a corner wearing the white and golden *salwar kameez* that Gary had picked for her just a few days ago. She did not have the heart to look at his body closely. With her head covered in a white veil, she sat stone-faced, watching everything from a distance.

The body was then taken to the cremation ground and shouldered by Gary's father and three other male relatives. It was placed on the pyre while the Sikh priest recited special prayers and sang hymns. As Gary's father lit the funeral pyre, tall and fierce red, yellow, and orange flames engulfed it. Soon all was finished—ashes to ashes, dust to dust.

One by one, all formalities were completed. The family visited the Gurudwara after cremation, where additional prayers and hymns were sung along with readings from *Sri Guru Granth Sahib Ji*. The next day, ashes were collected from the cremation ground and were scattered in a river by the Gurudwara. Layla walked through all ceremonies and formalities like a zombie.

Once everything was over, Layla didn't know what to do with her life or where to go. She stared all day at Gary's portrait, which now adorned the main wall of the living room. It was the portrait Layla had painted just a few months ago by the beach, while Gary had posed by his horse Top Gun. Layla did not know what to look forward to, but the Sandhu family eagerly awaited the birth of the little child who was going to be the one and only piece of their son in this world.

A month and a half later, a little girl was born to Layla, and the girl looked exactly like Gary. She was olive skinned with big brown eyes, black hair, and a sharp nose. They named her Jenna. Smiles returned to the Sandhu household once again. Gary's parents smiled and baby-talked with little Jenna all day long. They changed her diapers and bathed her in bubbles. They sang lullabies to her, rocked her to sleep, and quietly watched over her as she slept. They filled the entire house with plush baby toys, baby books, rattles, and teethers.

Layla's parents, upon hearing of Gary's demise and of the birth of their grandchild, decided to visit Layla. With heavy hearts, they paid their condolences to the family and then cradled little Jenna in their arms. They hugged her and kissed her as they showered her with tiny gifts, plush toys, and soft blankets. Both sets of grandparents played with little Jenna as she drooled and burped.

A few days later, Layla's parents asked Layla if she and Jenna wanted to go back with them to New York. Layla half-heartedly refused. Before leaving, her parents assured Layla that anytime she wanted to come back to New York to start afresh, they would be waiting for her and the baby with open arms. Layla thanked them for their love, generosity, and support as she hugged them and bid them goodbye.

After her parents left, Layla felt that she'd made a huge mistake. She and Jenna probably should have gone back to New York with them. There was nothing left to hold her interest in India, anyways. On the other hand, she did not want to take little Jenna away from Gary's parents; Jenna was all that they had. Layla was not even in a condition to provide as much love, care, and attention to the child as Gary's parents did. Layla felt sick, depressed, disillusioned, and perpetually heartbroken, and this could produce a negative influence on a child's mind. Layla deemed herself unfit to perform all motherly duties and responsibilities.

One thing emerged clear in her mind: Jenna was better off in her grandparents' care. The second thing Layla had to consider was herself. At this point in her life, Layla stood at crossroads and did not know which direction to choose. She did not want to go back to New York, she did not want to go back to Goa, and she did not want to live in Chandigarh. But she had to choose the lesser of evils. She chose Goa, but she would wait for little Jenna to turn 6 months old before making the move.

In the meantime, Layla meddled with spirituality. She wondered how Gary's parents seemed so calm and peaceful. They prayed at dawn and at twilight; they did not complain. When Layla asked Gary's father about his secret behind attainment of such peace, he said, "The secret is very simple, *beta ji*. It is simply saying *yes* to his order. Not fighting or resisting, but finding peace in his command. *Tera Bhana Meetha Lage* means whatever you have decided for me, O Lord, I find peace in it, I find it sweet."

It was not that simple for Layla. He gave Layla some spiritual books to read so she could find peace in his *Hukum* (order). Layla tried hard. Every morning and evening, she sat behind the *Sri Guru Granth Sahib* that was placed in the home, covered her head with a veil, and waved a long-handled horse-hair brush over the holy book while Gary's mother read *Sukhmani Sahib*. Layla read the English version of *Japuji Sahib* and *Sukhmani Sahib* (Sikh holy scriptures). She read the holy *Gita*, the Holy Bible, and the Buddhist scriptures. She practiced transcendental meditation and Vipassana. Nothing worked, and no peace descended upon her troubled mind. The storm inside her mind echoed louder and louder as she sat silently to meditate. Frustrated and angry, she cried and cried.

When baby Jenna turned 6 months old, Layla informed Gary's parents of her decision. They felt sad but did not want to tether Layla. After all, she was young and had her whole life ahead of her. They blessed her, kissed her, and let her go. "Keep visiting every few months, *beta ji*. Your mamma, Jenna, and I will miss you," said Gary's father in a strong voice and with tearful eyes.

Gary's mother hugged her and cried. Little Jenna crawled towards Layla, tugged on her skirt with her tiny hands, and mumbled, "Ma ... ma ... ma." Layla picked her up, hugged her, and cried. Then she strengthened her heart and left.

In June of 1977, Layla was back in Goa. She stood lifelessly in front of her dream house as she watched its moss-covered walls with listless eyes. Dark grey rain clouds loomed low in the sky, engulfing the house in an eerie melancholia. Tall, uncut grass had grown wild in the monsoon showers, shrouding the walkway that lead to the main door. Ants, grasshoppers, and earthworms had crept in every corner. Huge mosquitoes buzzed everywhere.

Layla heaved a deep, mournful sigh and then slowly tottered towards the front door. With a brass key, she unlocked the padlock that connected the ornate snake-shaped brass rings of the front door. Even the ornamental snakes seemed to be hissing at her. With a jerk, she slid open the door and plodded inside the house.

The walls grieved, every corner lamented, and every art piece seemed sinister. Large spiderwebs hung menacingly from wall corners, and termites infested the exposed wood. Gary's form lingered in open doorways, his loving words echoed in her ears, and the dusty floors spewed out images of Sophia's red blood. No, Layla could not live here. She called an *ayah* and got the house cleaned up. She locked it up again and decided to leave the keys with Gary's parents.

Layla then walked towards Belinda's house. Layla had received a few phone calls from Belinda and her other hippie friends to offer condolences on Gary's demise, but she knew nothing else of what was going on in Goa. She knocked on the door of Belinda's house a few times. There was no answer. She pounded on it, kicked, banged, and called out. "Belinda! Belinda, please open the door."

After 20 minutes of banging, Layla heard, a terrified voice say, "Who is it?"

"It's me, Layla. Open the door, please."

Belinda hastily unlocked the door and pulled in Layla by her arm. An emaciated Belinda hugged Layla, and the two cried. "I am so sorry, so sorry for you, my love," sniffled Belinda as her tears moistened Layla's neck.

"It's okay, Sweetheart," said Layla, rubbing Belinda's bony back. Belinda's frail flesh hung over her bones, which poked out from under her pale skin. Her tousled brunette head had not been combed for months, and her bangs fell down to her dry, powdery nose. Her eyes seemed like hollow pits, and her cheeks had sunken in. With mouth agape, Layla scanned Belinda from head to toe. Belinda's ghostly form terrified Layla, and she panicked. "What have you done to your beautiful self, Belinda?" she wailed. She broke down in hysterical tears of defeat and crumpled down on the grimy floor littered with drug paraphernalia.

"Hush, hush! Don't cry—they will hear us. The cops are prowling outside this house," whispered Belinda with her index finger placed against her chapped lips. "I have not stepped out of this house for past one month, or I would be dead by now in some rat-infested cell. I have also not slept for the past week. The moment I close my eyes, they will pounce on me!" A dog barked outside, and Belinda jumped in terror, scanning everything in the room.

"Who brings you drugs, water, food? Who pays your rent?" asked Layla.

"Alex does," answered Belinda as she manically searched the room

"Boy, oh boy!" uttered Layla as she shook her head.

Belinda had lost her marbles. Excessive drug usage, no sleep, and no food had triggered symptoms of schizophrenia in her, and she was now racing down the spiral path of death and destruction.

Layla talked Belinda into walking out with her. "Come with me, and I'll take you to a safe place, Belinda. Hide behind me; nobody can see you now," she whispered as she held Belinda's hand and walked her out of the house with a torchlight in her other hand. Belinda hid her face behind Layla's back and scurried behind her.

They walked down the paddy fields and the ravines. They walked up and over the boulders and dirt mounds, till they reached the paved road. Layla flagged down a taxi to the nearest hospital. Despite Belinda's loud cries and fits of resistance, Layla got her admitted. The doctor gave her a shot to put her to sleep. "You will be fine, Belinda. Trust me. I cannot lose you," whispered Layla as she caressed Belinda's head while she lay knocked out. The doctor later told Layla that for a day or two, Belinda would be fine in their care, but for proper treatment Belinda needed to get admitted into a detox centre in Bombay. Layla agreed. She slept beside Belinda's bed all night.

When Belinda woke up the next day, she was sweating and freezing. The doctor continually injected medication to keep her calm, drowsy, and asleep. Layla kissed Belinda on her forehead and said that she would be back soon. Belinda's gaze followed Layla out the door.

Layla decided to go back to her house and fetch some fresh clothing for Belinda. While walking back home, Layla saw two female figures dressed in orange and waving at her from a distance.

"Hola, Amiga!" shouted one.

"Hi there, Layla!" shouted another.

As Layla edged closer towards them, she recognized the faces. They were American Laura and Spanish Isabella. Layla hugged them both and invited them to her house. The three sat around Layla's Persian rug as they smoked bongs. Layla was so relieved to feel marijuana coursing through her bloodstream, relaxing her every limb, and calming down her anxious brain. Her body melted and sank inside the cushion and the rug. She had not felt this feeling for over a year. Suddenly the constant chatter and the loud noise inside her troubled mind had become silent. The grass seemed greener, and the sky seemed bluer. Her body felt light as a feather; she was ready to fly. "Bam Bam Bhole," shouted American Laura as she lit a chillum.

After 30 minutes of silent, blissful relaxation, Layla asked Laura and Isabella the secret to their orangeness. "It is Bhagwan," answered Spanish Isabella reverently.

"We now live in Poona, around Bhagwan's Ashram. We are just visiting Goa to collect our belongings," said American Laura in a wheeze as she let out a lungful of marijuana smoke. Then she continued in a clearer voice. "Read Bhagwan and listen to him. He will turn your world around," she said in an exhilarated tone as she slid one of Bhagwan's books and a few of Bhagwan's audio cassettes towards Layla.

For the next few days, Layla lay on the grass, smoked joints, and listened to Bhagwan. Bhagwan's hypnotic voice and mesmerising words left Layla spellbound. He talked about ecstasy, joy, laughter, bliss, and eternal dance. He talked about freedom from sorrow and suffering. He talked about eternal joy and laughter. Layla had suddenly stumbled upon what she had been looking for all her life. Layla cried tears of joy every morning and evening. This was it! She was leaving for Poona. The next morning, she got Belinda discharged from the hospital, and the two flew to Bombay. Layla got Belinda admitted into a reputed detox centre, hugged her, and bid her goodbye, assuring her that she would visit her every weekend till she got better. Belinda smiled and said goodbye, and her desolate gaze followed her friend to the door. Layla then left for Poona, a few hours' drive from Bombay, with new hopes and new dreams.

Chapter 14

There's a Killer on the Road

There's a killer on the road,
His brain is squirmin' like a toad.
Take a long holiday, let your children play,
If you give this man a ride, sweet family will die.
— *Jim Morrison*

Beads of sweat speckled Layla's forehead as she taxied through the narrow, winding, and bumpy road from Bombay to Poona in the hot and muggy month of June. Semi-naked sadhus with matted hair and horizontal lines of holy ash (*vibhuti*) smeared across their foreheads dotted the base of the Western Ghats, a long mountain range running along the western side of India. As the taxi started its bouncy climb up the Ghats, grey clouds loomed low over its rolling green hills. The narrow, uneven, and pothole-pitted road was suddenly overrun with gigantic trucks and lorries displaying vibrant artwork of peacocks, flowers, and deities in bright red, green, and orange. A few broken-down trucks were parked alongside the curvy road with big rocks shoved behind their tires to prevent them from rolling backwards. The driver twisted, turned, and slid with great expertise through a caravan of crawling trucks and lorries, and soon they were driving down the flat roads of Poona city.

"To Koregaon Park, please," said Layla, leafing through her diary in which she had written down the address given by Spanish Isabella.

"Okay, Madam," said the driver as he drove through the city streets bathed in pink and orange beams of the setting sun. The orange rays of the sun matched the orange robes of foreigners who strolled down the green roads in merry groups of twos and threes. Tiny stalls lined the sidewalk, displaying flowing orange robes in various styles and designs. The driver drove into a housing community of identical villas with flowered compounds, and he stopped in front of one. Layla clambered out of her taxi, paid the fare, and surveyed the area.

The houses seemed foreign, as did the residents. An orange couple stood locked in a lengthy embrace, blocking the gate of the house. Layla waited a minute or two, but the couple did not disentangle. Finally Layla cleared her throat and whispered, "Excuse me."

After deep, ecstatic sighs and long murmurs, they finally unlocked themselves from their loving hug and looked tenderly towards Layla. "Yes, beloved? How can I help you?" said the man in orange with a rapturous look on his face.

"Um, I am looking for Isabella. I guess this is her house," mumbled Layla, sounding a bit unsure.

"Oh! You mean Prem Sarita. She should be back any minute. We were waiting for her too," said the bubbly woman in orange with long, strawberry-blonde hair.

"Hola, Amiga!" shouted Spanish Isabella from a distance, jumping with excitement as she waved her dainty hands frantically. She hurried towards Layla with a wide smile on her pretty face. "I am so happy that you came, Love," she said, tossing her long black hair as she held Layla in a long embrace. After a few more hugs and kisses, she ushered everyone inside the house. The tall, lean orange man with shoulder-length blond hair, long sideburns, and a narrow face introduced himself as Krishna. The bubbly orange woman with a round face and strawberry-blonde hair was Meera.

The house with large windows had plants sprouting in every corner next to innumerable Buddha statues: the laughing Buddha, the reclining Buddha, the standing Buddha, and the meditating Buddha. Bhagwan's framed pictures hung everywhere in the living room, the dining room, the kitchen, and even along the winding staircase that lead to Layla's room. Spanish Isabella lead the way as she showed Layla to her room, which had a huge portrait of Bhagwan adorning the wall in front of her bed. Bhagwan, an Indian man with a long beard and twinkling eyes, sported a naughty, playful smile. Layla smiled back at the portrait as she slid her luggage in a corner. She was happy to notice Bhagwan's audio tapes and books neatly organised in a rack next to a large window by her bed. After a quick cold shower, Layla joined the others on the roof of the house.

American Laura, who was also now seated amongst orange friends, beamed at Layla. Laura and Layla exchanged a long hug, and then Layla squeezed in between a group of orange-clad friends with beaded malas who sprawled around the satin-covered mattresses, which were arranged in a circle. A pale quarter moon hung low in the sky amongst twinkling stars, lending its silvery shimmer to the meditators in orange, who sat ecstatically leaning against the satiny cushions. The soothing fragrance of night-blooming jasmine mixed with marijuana smoke soothed Layla's frayed nerves. They smoked bongs and weed-filled cigarettes as they talked about life and Bhagwan.

Between sobs and sniffles, Layla managed to relate the sad tale of her life, the loss of Gary, and her self-imposed separation from her daughter. As she trailed towards the sad end of her story, she unleashed a river of tears. Isabella, Laura, and Meera engulfed Layla in a warm hug as she wept, caressing her back with occasional murmurs. "You have come home, beloved, and you will be healed," announced Krishna in his melodious French accent as he flailed his lanky arms in rapture. "Bhagwan works in mysterious ways!" He closed his eyes and shook his tousled head of blond hair side to side in a reverent fashion. "Whatever happened in your life was a series of difficult steps to lead you to your heaven—here, close to Bhagwan." He smiled tenderly as he edged closer to Layla and held her in an overwhelmingly long, emotional hug. Then he inched away with a tuneful murmur of "Mmm..." and added softly and passionately, "I was so tired of peeling potatoes and onions, with my teary eyes, in one of the chic restaurants of Paris day and night. Then I stumbled upon Bhagwan. That day, my life changed. I left that monotonous and meaningless life behind me in France, packed my bags, and came to Bhagwan's ashram. Now, every day of my life is full of joy, love, laughter, and dance. I am so blessed to be here, so happy—and so will you be, Layla." He placed his hands tenderly over his heart and bent his head low in reverence. Layla edged closer to him and whispered a thank-you with a brief hug.

Bubbly Meera, who sat huddled in a corner, suddenly broke out in an overwhelming display of emotion. "And I was so tired of selling lingerie behind the counters of a department store in New York, and getting dumped by sleazy boyfriends every fortnight, that I was at the brink of a breakdown. Had I not found Bhagwan, I would have *died*!" she wailed as she buried her face in a satiny cushion. Layla, Laura, and Krishna inched closer to her with dewy eyes and engulfed her in a compassionate hug. "Mmm," they murmured as they caressed her back and ran their fingers through her long hair.

For the rest of the night, one by one, they all shared their woes, sorrows, and joys over bongs and weed until they gradually lay down on the mattresses after emotional exhaustion and fell sound asleep under the starlit sky, with their arms and legs wrapped around one another.

In the middle of the night, feeling scratchy and itchy, Layla woke up to the loud buzzing of the mosquitoes next to her ear. With a flap of a hand, she waved them away. As she sat up, she realized that she was covered in mosquito bites. She moved aside a leg and an arm and staggered out of the mattress area, tottering her way down to her room. She lay her weary head on a downy pillow, lit up a joint, wore her headphones, and turned on Bhagwan's tape. Bhagwan started speaking in a slow and captivating voice, and his every word and sentence left Layla enraptured and spell bound. She felt a healing inside her aching heart like she had never felt before. It seemed to her that Bhagwan was speaking directly to her. "Surrender to me, and you will be transformed. This is my promise," murmured Bhagwan in Layla's ears. Layla was jumping out of her skin to surrender. She wanted to run to Bhagwan, throw herself on his altar, and surrender unto him. But she had to wait till dawn.

As Layla lay blissed out and listening to Bhagwan, the doorbell rang. Layla sat up, startled. *It is 3:30 a.m.—who can it be?* she wondered. *Oh, Leonardo!* She remembered a moment later. Isabella had mentioned last night that her husband, Handsome Leonardo, was getting back from Italy in the morning. Layla clambered out of her bed, rubbed her eyes, staggered towards the front door, and slid open the bolt.

"Ciao, Bella!" greeted Handsome Leonardo cheerfully as he kissed Layla on both sides of her cheeks. "I am so happy to see you here." He beamed as he glided inside. A handsome, medium-statured man with blue eyes and sandy-brown, shoulder-length hair followed him. "Meet my cousin. Riccardo Romano. We travelled together from Italy," said Leonardo as he introduced the two. The two greeted one another with slight smiles and friendly glances. "Where is my wifey dear?" asked Leonardo as he craned his neck and surveyed the house.

"Oh! Isabella is sleeping on the roof with a couple of orange friends," replied Layla.

"Okay, dear. You go back to sleep, please. I will take care of everything," said Leonardo in his strong Italian accent.

At 5:00 a.m., Layla was woken up by loud pounding on the door. It was Spanish Isabella. "Layla, wake up! It's time to get ready to go to the ashram," she shouted.

Layla opened the door. "Did you meet Leonardo? He's back," Layla said as she carefully scanned the dainty and pretty Isabella, who stood in the doorway freshly bathed and clothed in a crisp, new set of stylish, backless orange robes. "Boy, oh boy! You are up and ready to embrace the day," Layla noted with a bright smile.

"Yes, I am, Amiga," Isabella replied. "I have this fresh set of orange robes for you. It is Laura's. I guess it will fit you. Take a quick shower and get ready. Later in the day, we will do some robe shopping for you." Isabella handed Layla the orange robe.

Layla took a shower, changed, and stood a moment in front of the mirror. She admired herself while wearing the fashionable, flowing, loose-fitted, strapless orange robe. She missed the beaded mala around her neck. Suddenly her eyes welled up with tears. She missed Gary. She missed his compliments and kisses he showered upon her each time she wore something new. She missed him utterly. She cried.

Isabella heard her and rushed inside. She wrapped a loving arm around Layla and caressed her back and hair. "It's okay, Love. It's okay. You'll be fine, you'll be healed," whispered Isabella in Layla's ear. Layla wiped her tears and splashed water on her face.

Layla, Spanish Isabella, American Laura, Krishna, and Meera sat around a Japanese table, sipping on their steaming hot cups of Brazilian coffee, when they heard a soft male voice call from behind. "May I join you?" asked Riccardo in his melodious Italian accent.

"Yes, of course, Amigo! Join in," said Isabella gleefully pulling out a chair for Riccardo. She continued as she turned her head towards Krishna. "Krishna, could you please lend him your orange robe?"

"Yes, of course," said Krishna. "Have you ever listened to Bhagwan, Riccardo?" he asked when he returned with an orange robe, handing it over to Riccardo.

"No, I have not, but I am keen and would like to experiment," answered Riccardo with one eye on Layla.

Riccardo and Leonardo were first cousins, and they shared the same business. They smuggled heroin and hash to Western countries. They had a large network spread over Pakistan, Afghanistan, India, and Europe. Leonardo had his base in Goa but now had bought a house in Poona due to his wife's love for Bhagwan. In Goa, many hippies worked under Leonardo and acted as drug mules by transporting illegal drugs to Western countries, either by swallowing them or concealing them in their body cavities. The gang's drug-smuggling techniques changed every six months, to keep police from becoming aware of their ways. The latest racket they'd organised was the export of heroin hidden creatively inside crates of chocolate eggs. The run was a huge success. Riccardo and Leonardo had just returned from Italy after attaining great success in their business, and they were now working on their next assignment. Isabella was well aware of her husband's business, but she stayed away from any active involvement in it. She loved her husband, and that was all that mattered to her.

The rising orange sun peeked out of the eastern sky, emitting soft golden rays that slowly replaced the blues and purples of the twilight sky. Birds tweeted around bushes, and a whizzing crow cawed on its way to a nearby branch as Layla and her friends rode to the ashram on two separate rickshaws. Orange people dotted the green sidewalks leading to the ashram, locked in eternal hugs. The rickshaws jolted on the road that ran in between of two massive blocks of black buildings shrouded in lush greenery. Layla and her orange friends climbed down the rickshaws, and suddenly the hugging erupted. Isabella (aka Sarita), Krishna, and Meera leisurely and patiently hugged every single orange person they met on their way to the welcome centre. The lengthy hugs were accompanied by long murmurs of "Mmm" followed by clenching and squeezing each other tightly before disentangling themselves.

Layla and Riccardo trailed behind their orange friends, surveyed the scene, and exchanged friendly glances. The interior of the ashram was lush green, with lofty green trees that accented the shiny black marble of the building. Bright flowers blossomed in patches around a narrow stream that rippled through its rolling green hillocks. A magnificently serene, white marble Buddha statue sat in peace, towering over the splendid green and black of the ashram. Layla felt warmth in her heart, as well as the coolness of the marble floor on her bare feet.

As Layla looked around, she noticed young Westerners in orange strolling down the green paths against the backdrop of black marble structures. They were hand in hand and beaming peaceful smiles. Couples stood locked in lengthy embraces, and a few lounged on the lush lawn. A man sat in Buddha pose with closed eyes, detached from his surroundings. A woman danced ecstatically with raised arms. A man hugged a tree and stood motionless. The ashram was full of young dreamers and hairy blondes keen to unravel the spiritual mysteries of the East, taught by an Indian guru who possessed spiritual intelligence and a deep understanding of the Western mind.

After completing the registration formalities at the main reception, the group walked through "the Gateless Gate" and headed towards the Buddha Hall. Two women were posted outside the hall to sniff the guests, in order to check them for any traces of perfumes and scents. They took deep whiffs of Layla's hair and robe before letting her step inside the magnificent marble hall. The meditation hall comprised of 10,000 square feet of marble floor constructed as a raised, round platform with a domed green canvas canopy for a roof. It was without walls, leaving it open to the rich green of lush plants, flowers, and bamboos trees.

Bhagwan arrived at 6:00 a.m. sharp in his shiny white Rolls Royce, covering a path of 150 metres from his residence of Lao Tzu to the Meditation Hall to deliver his morning discourse. Sannyasins lined his path dressed in colours of the rising sun. In an ocean of red, peach, and orange, they danced and swayed their arms to welcome him. A few stood silently with palms pressed together as tears of gratitude brimmed in their eyes. Bhagwan, wearing a long and fancy robe, walked slowly towards the platform at the head of the hall with his palms folded together. As he stood on the podium facing his disciples and visitors, he gave a slow bow and then took a seat on his pagoda.

Layla sat in silent rapture with palms pressed together. She closed eyes as she listened to Bhagwan speak. Bhagwan talked of his dream of bringing Gautama the Buddha and Zorba the Greek together in his disciples. "I want my disciple to be Zorba the Buddha," he said. "Man is both the soul and the body together. Both have to be satisfied, the soul as well as the body."

It clicked. "Yes!" sighed Layla, captivated by Bhagwan's entrancing words. Layla had read holy scriptures that preached restraint, renunciation, and a saintly way of leading a serious and sombre life devoid of laughter and joy. This was the first time she had heard a guru preach dance, celebration, and laughter.

Bhagwan's disciples were free to indulge, though with mindfulness. "Any vain activity performed with mindfulness drops away by itself," Bhagwan would often say. Only drugs and non-vegetarian food were banned in the ashram, but everything else was okay, including a Zen bar and a smoking temple. Layla could finally laugh, dance, and celebrate her way to glittery skies and heavens above. She compared the sad, thin, and pale disciples of strict gurus and the addicted, hedonist hippies of Goa to the fit, happy, jovial, and healthy disciples of Bhagwan. A perfect balance? Yes! This was what she had been looking for, and she had found it!

After Bhagwan left, Layla danced. She hugged people she did not know. She cried tears of joy. She hugged Isabella, Krishna, Meera, Laura, and Riccardo. There was something different about her hug with Riccardo. A strange attraction lingered between the two. Layla tried half-heartedly to disentangle herself from his embrace, but she couldn't. She needed someone to hold on to; she needed a shoulder to cry on. So she held on to him, clutching on to his sleeve like a lost child. She felt his heart beat against hers, and suddenly she found comfort and solace as he pressed her tighter against his chest, squeezed her shoulder, and breathed softly in her ear.

Chapter 15
Into This World We're Thrown

Riders on the storm,
Into this house we're born,
Into this world we're thrown,
Like a dog without a bone,
An actor out on loan.

—Jim Morrison

The next day, Layla made an appointment at the ashram office to take *sannyas* (disciplehood). At 6:00 p.m., Layla and a few other orange-clad, hairy dreamers entered the meditation hall after being proclaimed scent-free by the sniffing staff. Layla sat on the marble floor with folded palms, waiting for Bhagwan. She felt flurries of excitement grow inside her stomach in anticipation of her new spiritual life.

Finally Bhagwan entered with palms pressed together, wearing his shiny white robe. He seated himself on a fancy chair placed on the podium. After addressing the orange ocean falling in waves at his feet, he called the *sannyas* aspirants one by one. When Layla's turn came, she nervously shambled her way to Bhagwan. She kneeled before the master with folded palms as he placed a mala (a necklace of 108 rosewood beads with Bhagwan's picture) around her neck and placed his thumb between her eyebrows (the third-eye chakra). Layla felt Bhagwan's energy run through her body like a divine shock. "From now on, your name will be Ma Prem Leela," announced Bhagwan. "It means 'love with divine play.'" Layla quivered in rapture with tears of gratitude streaming down her cheeks. The orange-robed, mala-ridden sannyasins danced around her wildly with flaying arms and rolling heads; they whirled and swayed their hands in praise of the universe.

After the ceremony, Layla was smothered in hugs and kisses by the zealous sannyasins, including Isabella, Laura, Krishna, and Meera, congratulating her on her new life as an orange person. To celebrate Layla's first evening as a *sannyasin*, the group headed towards hotel Blue Diamond, a five-star joint that was a five-minute walk from the ashram. They ran into Leonardo and Riccardo at the hotel bar and joined them after a lavish exchange of hugs and kisses. They toasted and tinkled their wine glasses at the bar by the pool, and they cheered, "To Ma Prem Leela." The hotel was full of orange-clothed sannyasins flaunting their spiritual rebellion to the conventional world. They hung around in the lobby, lounged in the bar, and reclined by the pool wearing long *malas* with orange bikinis and trunks.

Isabella, Laura, Krishna, and Meera decided to leave after a few drinks, in preparation of participating in an encounter group organised by a veteran *sannyasin*. "Come along, join in. It will do you good," said Isabella with a slight jerk of her head as she nudged Layla, who sat with her arm on the table.

"No, thank you. I have had enough for the day and need some quiet time to reflect on life," stated Layla complacently. She paused for a moment and then added, "But I will surely join in tomorrow, if that's okay."

"Yes, of course, Amiga! Take your time and relax today," assured Isabella as she patted Layla on the shoulder. Then she pushed back her chair and stood up to leave, followed by the others. "Adios, Amiga." Isabella kissed her.

"Au revoir," Krishna said with a wave.

"See ya later," Laura said while hugging her.

Leonardo ran into a group of friends at the hotel and joined them.

Riccardo sat motionless by Layla's side. "Do you mind if I stick around with you?" he asked in a soft whisper as he leaned over the table towards Layla.

"No, I don't mind, Riccardo," answered Layla with listless eyes and a slight smile. Riccardo beamed and ordered a bottle of wine. Over their drinks, Layla rambled, ranted, laughed, and cried, oblivious of Riccardo's presence. Riccardo listened silently and patiently.

Once Layla was done with her catharsis, Riccardo wrapped his arm around her shoulder, and she lay her weary head on his. He wiped her tears and murmured, "It's okay, Love. It's okay."

Under the light of a shimmery moon and a light drizzle, they walked homewards, with Riccardo's right arm resting across Layla's shoulder. Under a colossal banyan tree, Riccardo stopped and turned to face Layla. The large, glossy, green, dewy leaves of the banyan stooped low over the two and engulfed them in a green mist as Riccardo held Layla's hand in his, looked deep into her wavering blue eyes, and then wrapped her in a hug. An auto rickshaw *phut-phutted* past them as he kissed her lips.

A pleasant surprise awaited Layla as she and Riccardo entered the house. A small group of orange friends had gathered on the roof to celebrate Layla's sannyas day. People with long malas and stylish orange clothes lounged around satin-covered mattresses and cushions. They wore orange halter and strapless dresses, orange maxis, orange overalls, orange Chinese pants, and orange silk vests as they mingled, laughed, cried, hugged, kissed, and snuggled. They smoked weed from long cigarettes and fancy bongs, and they danced and swayed to the beats of African drums. Layla sipped on a punch prepared by Riccardo.

When Layla started floating in the air, she realised that the punch had been spiked with LSD. She saw Lord Shiva dance on the moon as trees and plants talked to her. The universe throbbed with one heartbeat as she, he, the plants, the trees, the animals, the moon, and the stars melted into one. Colours Layla had never seen before dyed the universe in various shades of fluorescent greens, pinks, and purples. Brightly-coloured geometrical patterns danced and pulsated in everything, living and nonliving. Mosquitoes whispered poetry of love in Layla's ears as she whirled along with the planets that spun and sang the eternal song of *Om*. Gary looked at Layla through Riccardo's eyes, and suddenly Gary and Riccardo had merged into one. It was Gary's soul in Riccardo's body when Layla and Riccardo made love that starry, magical night.

The next morning, Layla woke up feeling wretched. What had she done? She wanted to shout, scream, yell, bellow, and bawl. Riccardo was still fast asleep when she bathed and got dressed to go to the ashram with Isabella and Laura. She had heard a lot about dynamic meditation, but this was the first time she was going to try it out. The meditation had been specifically devised by Bhagwan, keeping in mind the repressive nature of the Western mind. Bhagwan believed in the safe release of all anger, emotion, and repression in order to transcend it. Doctors, psychiatrists, and psychologists from Europe and America became Sannyasins and introduced encounter groups, bioenergetics, Gestalt therapies, primal scream therapies, and more into the ashram. Bhagwan created a unique blend of Western radical therapies mixed with age-old, traditional meditations of the East. These therapies cum meditations suited the modern mind, which was overwhelmed with stress and emotion, and they gave individuals a chance to express and unload before moving into silence.

Daylight crawled over the horizon as Layla, Isabella, and Laura bounced their way to the ashram on a rickshaw. Layla maintained silence throughout the short, bumpy ride. She was overwhelmed with mixed emotions of fear, disgust, anger, vulnerability and self-pity. That morning in the Buddha Hall, her feet burnt with rage even on the cold white marble floor of the hall. She listened carefully to the meditation instructions, wore a blindfold over her eyes, and then followed. During the first stage, she breathed fast and chaotically along with hundreds of others dressed in orange. Their malas flapped noisily against their chests as they shook their torso back and forth in an effort to throw out their breath. This first stage was to release all old emotional knots and blocks in the body, Bhagwan had explained. During the second stage, she let go and released all emotion. She laughed, shrieked, hurled abuses in the air, screamed, shouted, stomped her feet on the ground, and cried like a helpless child.

During the third stage, she jumped up and down with raised arms, shouting, "Hoo, hoo." Bhagwan said this sound would hit the sex centre and stir the dormant Kundalini energy that lay coiled and inactive at the bottom of the spine. Layla shouted and jumped with all her energy till an instructor's voice shouted to stop. Everyone froze. During the fourth stage, Layla stood still with arms still raised as she felt the Kundalini uncoil and rise upwards. Her mental and physical exhaustion ran down the side of her temple in the form of a blob of sweat that fell on the floor with a splat while she stood motionless. Layla's anger was released, and all was now silent and clear. She felt light, like a feather floating in a gentle breeze as she slowly danced during the last stage of the meditation.

Layla walked out of the Buddha Hall feeling calm and silent. As she walked towards the shoe rack to collect her sandals, she saw Riccardo standing below the sign that read, "Beloveds, please leave your shoes and minds behind." Layla smiled as she picked up her sandals, but she decided to leave her mind behind. Riccardo opened up his arms and wrapped Layla in a hug. She surrendered and hugged him back. "We can be friends, can't we, *amore mio?*" Riccardo whispered softly in Layla's ear. Layla nodded a thoughtful yes. "Let's go grab some breakfast," he suggested as he wrapped an arm around Layla.

"I need to shower first. I am too sweaty," said Layla. The two walked towards the fancy black wooden showers in the ashram, which were open on the top and surrounded by thick green foliage. Branches laden with flowers stooped over Layla's head as she showered under a stream of cold water. Layla closed her eyes gently and dealt with her emotions. What had angered her? What was Riccardo's fault? Was it his fault to listen to her while she cried her heart out? No, it was not; he was simply being kind. Neither did he force himself upon her physically. Riccardo was not to be blamed if she had seen Gary's soul inside his body. Riccardo had in fact provided her with an outlet to heal her wounds. Today she felt a bit better, though mostly because of Bhagwan. There was no way she could possibly deny this fact.

A knock on the wooden bathroom door broke Layla out of her reasoning of the situation. "May I join you, *amore mio*?" requested Riccardo. Layla opened the door to let in Riccardo. She closed her eyes and dropped her inhibitions and armour as the cold water swept away all her fears and doubts. The two showered with flower-laden branches swaying over them.

For breakfast, they walked over to Vrindavan, the ashram cafeteria. Nestled between flowery trees and surrounded by wooden frames laden with climbing and trailing vines, the cafeteria, with its self-service counters, seemed like an open-air American fast food joint set amidst a lush, green, flowery Japanese garden. Layla and Riccardo grabbed trays and walked along the counters, picking up their choices for a gourmet continental breakfast. They seated themselves on a corner table under a tree with bright pink flowers. Birds perched on the flowery branches and chirped as the two ate breakfast in reflective silence.

Mas and Swamis dressed in orange robes, with beaded malas hanging around their necks, filled the tables all around the cafeteria.

They chattered and prattled about their meditative experiences under the swaying branches of the trees. A blonde Ma seated on a neighbouring table had just had a Kundalini awakening this morning. A golden-haired Swami seated on the front table had seen his past seven lives during a meditative insight last evening. A brunette Ma seated on a table on the right felt that her third eye was suddenly beginning to open. She started shaking and vibrating with the universal force that was trying to open her third eye while the surrounding sannyasins gently held her and walked her over to a quieter place more suitable for a third-eye opening experience.

Layla and Riccardo smiled at one another as they walked over to a row of tea urns and poured themselves some lemon grass tea. Over their cups of tea, they talked. Riccardo expressed his love for Layla, and Layla expressed her unpreparedness to get into a relationship. "I understand, *amore mio*. Just take me as a friend for now, if nothing else. I will wait till you feel better, and till you feel that I am worthy of your love," said Riccardo with an earnest look in his eyes as he leaned over the table. He held Layla's hand with his left hand and moved his right hand frantically in an up-and-down motion, with its fingertips brought together in an Italian gesture, as he spoke. His sandy-brown, shoulder-length, silky hair glimmered in the sun as Layla looked into his compelling blue eyes.

Layla heaved a deep sigh, smiled, and then wrapped her arms around him "You are a lovely person Riccardo. Thank you for being around," she whispered in his ear as the two hugged.

Riccardo beamed with joy, raised his arms up in the air, and shouted "Woo hoo!"

They walked over to the ashram post office because Layla wanted to make a trunk call to the Bombay detox centre to talk to Belinda. She circled her index finger around the rotary dial and waited to get connected. "May I speak with Belinda or her doctor?" she asked. Her jaw dropped as she listened with the phone handle pressed against her ear. "She *what*?" Layla shrieked. She placed the handle down and stood motionless as tears trickled down her cheeks. "Belinda is gone too," she uttered, staring into space as she slumped against the wall and crumpled down to the floor. Riccardo held her by the shoulders as she continued. "Belinda tried to run away from the detox centre in a disoriented frame of mind. She was run over by a truck when she tried to cross a busy street, trying to evade the hospital staff who followed her." Layla broke down in hysterical tears. "I killed Belinda! I killed my best friend! Why did I ever bring her to Bombay? Why did I not leave her behind in Goa?" Riccardo hugged Layla and caressed her as she wailed in deep pain.

Layla, Riccardo, Handsome Leonardo, Spanish Isabella, and American Laura travelled to Bombay to claim Belinda's body, which lay in a morgue. After performing the last rites with heavy hearts, they returned to Poona. Layla felt utterly alone in this world. She called Chandigarh twice a week to talk to Jenna and to Gary's parents. She called her own parents from time to time. She meditated daily and tried to keep Riccardo at bay. She was not ready for any commitment and did not want to form any new attachments. Her older attachments had taken a toll on her. Belinda's death to Layla was the straw that broke the camel's back. Life seemed too short and uncertain because the dark shadow of death lingered everywhere, mocking her. Only Bhagwan's words provided solace to her bleeding heart. Bhagwan talked of transitory nature of all life, forms, and relationships. She listened to Bhagwan all day and night as she meditated daily and participated in therapies and groups.

A month went by as she steeped in reflection, meditation, sadness, and mourning. Layla started feeling sick and nauseous. Assuming that she must have contracted food poisoning, she decided to go to the doctor. "You are pregnant," announced the doctor. Layla's world shattered. She was not ready for this. She talked to Riccardo, who suggested abortion. "I do not believe in abortion!" yelled Layla, her eyes ablaze with anger. "If the universe has sent this life in my womb, there must be a reason and purpose behind it. This child *will* take birth."

"I am ok with your decision, *amore mio*. It's just that I am worried about you. You are not in a condition to take care of this child. As you know, I stay extremely busy with my work, and I am always hopping from country to country. Are you sure you will be able to look after this child?" pressed Riccardo.

"The universe will look after this child, if I am unable to," mumbled Layla as she lay her weary head on Riccardo's shoulder.

Months rolled by. Layla became a popular and favoured figure in the ashram. She was assigned duties and responsibilities by the staff, and she actively spread Bhagwan's message to the world. Riccardo bought a house close to Isabella and Leonardo's house, and Layla moved in with him. One fine morning, a blue-eyed baby boy was born to Layla and Riccardo. They named him Jovan.

Chapter 16

End of the Night

Take the highway to the end of the night,
End of the night, end of the night.
Take a journey to the bright midnight,
End of the night, end of the night.

—*Jim Morrison*

When Jovan was one week old, Layla took an appointment with Bhagwan for a special *darshan* (meeting). She wrapped Jovan in a fuzzy orange blanket, meandered through the flowery trees and hanging vines of the black Ashram building, and then scurried to Bhagwan's residence. She patiently waited outside the gates till she was signalled to come in. After passing the customary sniffing test, she entered the sacred sanctum and was welcomed by Bhagwan, who was sitting in a dentist's chair. "Come in, Prem Leela," he greeted with a smile.

Layla kneeled reverently in front of Bhagwan and placed the cooing and cawing infant at his feet. "Bhagwan, I have placed him in your care. Kindly bless him and take him under your wing," requested Layla with brimming eyes and folded palms.

Bhagwan blessed Layla and the child. "Do not worry about the child, Leela. The universe will take care of him," affirmed Bhagwan with a complacent gaze. "You should allow him to bloom and grow in the ashram as you progress on your own spiritual path. The child is no longer your responsibility; the universe is looking after him." Layla fell at Bhagwan's feet in gratitude as she mentally freed herself from Jovan's responsibility.

Layla's parents flew down from New York to meet their grandson. They were happy to hold the little, blue-eyed boy in their arms, who snuggled close to their chests. They requested Layla permit them to take baby Jovan along with them to New York because they thought the ashram was not the right place for the boy's growth. Layla refused and argued that the boy was being very well looked after. Layla's parents returned to New York with heavy hearts.

A couple of months later, Layla travelled to Chandigarh to see Jenna and to introduce her to her baby brother. Layla had never worried about Jenna. During her pregnancy, Layla had made a few trips to Chandigarh to see her daughter and Gary's parents, and she couldn't have been better satisfied. Jenna was living the coddled, pampered life of a princess. The Sandhu family and a well-trained staff tended after her 24 hours a day. Gary's parents were also happy to know that Layla had found someone to spend her life with, and they had given her their blessings.

The Sandhu family welcomed Layla and her newborn. Jenna, now 2 years old, played with little Jovan. She shared her toys with him and cried to have him in her lap. Along with her mommy, she pulled silly faces at him to make him laugh, and she sang lullabies to him when he felt sleepy. Little Jovan returned Jenna's affection with equal vigour. He giggled, played, and kicked his legs in the air as she swung a soft toy over his face, and he laughed the most in her company. Layla was happy to see the special bond brother and sister shared.

Back in Poona, life continued for Layla, dyed in the colour orange. Jovan crawled, cried, stumbled, and tottered his way to the age of 2 while his mommy gazed at the stars above and his daddy dodged the police the world over. Soon after moving in with Riccardo, Layla had become aware of his mighty business. Heroin lay in abundance around the house, hidden in secret places, inviting Layla to take a little sniff of the heavens—a shortcut to the valley of gods.

The earth and its people did not interest Layla anymore. Riccardo was nothing more than an arrangement to keep her life from falling apart; there never was any love between the two. The only gratification she received from this relationship was the acknowledgement of the fact that she had provided Jovan with a "daddy." Jenna was being well looked after by her grandparents, and Jovan was looked after by the universe. Layla was finally free to experiment, to indulge, to lose everything if she had to in her spiritual quest.

Layla had had many spiritual experiences during her meditation sessions laced with marijuana. She had flown out of her body and floated above the earth. She had spoken to God and seen the planets spin beneath her. She had seen her own body lying on a mattress on the roof of the house, passed out, while she flew around the universe. She knew that she was more than a body, so the body did not matter to her anymore. There was nothing left to lose but her lower self. She desired to fly high in the sky.

One day Riccardo and Leonardo sat in the living room of their home sniffing heroin, to check it for quality. Layla walked in and sat beside them while little Jovan entertained himself by tossing and turning the sealed packets of heroin that were lying in an open suitcase. Riccardo took a sniff and glanced at Layla, who watched him keenly. "You want to try it, *amore mio?*" offered Riccardo, extending a mirror with neatly arranged lines of the powder and a rolled-up bill.

Layla extended her eager nose and sniffed. Her body and mind eased and relaxed as she reclined back and allowed the rush to sweep over her. A feeling of euphoria emanated from the heart centre of her body, accompanied by a feeling of tingling warmth. A formless, spiritual lover descended upon her. Layla had heard many times that one did not need a physical lover when one sniffed heroin, but she was experiencing it firsthand for the very first time.

She was falling in love with someone she could not see or describe, but she could feel it. A sublime feeling of contentment, comfort, and joy engulfed her; all was suddenly right with the world. Heroin had instantly swept away all her mental torments and tribulations, and peace descended upon her soul. She was happy. The entire load that had been weighing her down for years had been magically lifted up, and she felt light and free to fly.

From that day onwards, there was no looking back for Layla. The miraculous powder had taken over her life. Her days passed steeped in heroin contentment, coupled with meditative therapies. Riccardo could not care less. He was busy travelling the world and healing its troubled souls by selling them the potent powder with supernatural powers. Then one morning, he was caught at the Delhi Airport in possession of eight kilograms of heroin. He was moved to the Tihar jail, where he continued his business with help from his network, and a little help from an unwilling Layla, who complained yet complied as if possessed by some unknown force. Her eyes were set on higher heavens, and she did not pay much attention to the trivialities and petty matters of daily life.

Jovan grew up stumbling, staggering, and falling in various hands. Instead of one mother, he had many orange-clad mums who looked after the mutual *sannyasin* kids in rotation while their mothers worked in the ashram, organising meditation sessions and spreading Bhagwan's work. Along with orange mums, Jovan also had Lakshmi, the *ayah*, at home; she cooked, fed, and clothed Jovan, as well as put him to bed every night. Lakshmi and her daughter, Meera, lived in the servants' quarters of the house. Meera, who was almost the same age as Jovan, was a constant companion to him. Jovan also had another companion, his white and fluffy Westie, Wolfie, who played, bounced, slurped, and slobbered all over Jovan. Lakshmi narrated stories to Jovan at bedtime while Wolfie lay beside Jovan's bed. Jovan listened with his eye on the door, waiting for his mommy to return. She invariably returned after midnight when Jovan was fast asleep.

Jovan went to the ashram school with other *sannyasin* children. Lakshmi fed him breakfast, packed him lunch, and put him on a rickshaw shared with other orange kids while Mommy meditated and performed her duties in the ashram. Wolfie invariably ran behind his rickshaw till Jovan shooed him back home. In school, Jovan had orange-clad, long-haired teachers with beaded malas hanging around their necks, and they taught him Math and English. After school, the children walked to the ashram and played quietly in its maze of lush gardens, talking in whispers and giggling, trying to catch their mommies' eyes when the women occasionally waved at them from a distance while conducting groups and sessions.

Once Mommy was finished with her duties of the day and was free to meditate in the evening, Jovan would occasionally join her in the Buddha Hall for energy darshan. Sannyasins in orange gathered on the marble floor of the auditorium. A music band tuned their guitars and other musical instruments on an elevated platform to one side. Music blared in the hall as the band played on guitars, tambourines, and drums. Bhagwan began his energy darshan by placing his thumb firmly onto Sannyasins' foreheads as they kneeled at his feet. As Bhagwan's energy travelled through their bodies, they trembled and twitched with ecstatic joy while designated sannyasin women with flowing robes whirled around them with raised arms. Sannyasins who gathered in the hall for darshan danced, swayed, or sat silently with closed eyes on the round marble floor. Jovan would either curl up in his mommy's lap or lie beside her with his head on a cushion. The blasting music could not keep him from drifting into his world of dreams, in which he swung across the buildings of New York along with Spiderman and played in the park with Mommy, Daddy, and Jenna.

Those lucky nights when Mommy came home early, she would play and hum along with Jim Morrison or Scott McKenzie's music, or she'd listen to the English version of the *Bhagavad Gita* and meditate. Jovan had grown to remember all of the band's songs and the summary of the *Bhagavad Gita* by heart. Many times Mommy would lock herself in her room, lie on her bed, and listen to Bhagwan while the marijuana fog that escaped from the narrow opening under the door filled up the entire house. Lakshmi and Meera would cough, and Jovan would inhale and bask in the familiar fragrance.

Whenever Mommy was home, the house always filled up with orange people. They would often hold groups either inside the house or on its roof. Jovan, who tried to sleep, would either hear people laughing or crying, and he'd plug his ears. A couple of times he had sneaked inside the room where Mommy's group meditated, and he'd peeked from behind a couch. He saw a group of semi-naked people wearing blindfolds and sitting in a circle. They played something somewhat similar to the game of Truth or Dare. They talked one at a time, trying to be as truthful as possible about themselves and their emotions. After sharing, they hugged, cried, laughed, jumped, and acted like a toddler or an animal. Basically, they did and said whatever they felt like, allowing their suppressed emotions to surface without any shame or guilt. Jovan would then sneak back out of the room and incorporate the stolen knowledge of Bhagwan's meditations in his playtime.

Days rolled into months, and months turned into years. Jovan was now 7 years old. He had grown up visiting his father in jail, his sister in Chandigarh, and his mother in the ashram. He identified himself as an orange child, raised by the rebellious meditators in orange who had given up on set ways of life and were creating a new world full of love and free of possession and expectation.

Jovan clutched his teddy bear, hugged Wolfie, and sulked to sleep many times, longing for a normal mommy and daddy, for a normal life that he had seen only in movies. He longed to live with his parents and sister under one roof. He longed for a family holiday, a circus, a movie, a picnic, a walk in a park. Many times when Mommy would come home early, Jovan would try to talk to her at bedtime. She would lie beside him and pass out while he expressed his wishes, dreams, and desires. He would shake her and try to wake her up, but when she wouldn't respond, he would give up on her and share his feelings with the star tattoo engraved on her arm. The star listened. Jovan would wipe his tears on the star's face as he moped and sobbed himself to sleep.

Layla was winding down the path of addiction at a fast speed. When she had started, she had been fooled by the feeling that she had power over the drug and could give up on it whenever she wanted to, but her various, half-hearted attempts on giving up had proved that she could not. She had started with heroin, but along the way she had also started dabbling with cocaine and other hallucinogens like LSD. She was now addicted and could not go a day without sniffing the powder. However, she still had hope of recovery because she had not yet lost her marbles like Belinda, Juan, and many others.

One night after dropping acid, Layla started hallucinating. She saw God, who called her to the moon along with Jovan. She picked up Jovan from his bed while he was fast asleep, placed him in the backseat of the car, and started driving in the dead of the night. "Where are we going, Mommy?" mumbled Jovan as he rubbed his eyes.

"To the moon, Dear," she answered as she cranked up "End of the Night" and sang along with it. "Take the highway to the end of the night ... take a journey to the bright midnight," she chanted loudly as Jovan cried in the backseat. She drove down the highway, blinded by the bright colours of the drug that guided her to follow along the bright and whirly tunnel, till she crashed in a tree and passed out with her head against the steering. Jovan managed to step out of the car, crying his lungs out. He flagged down a car that called an ambulance, and the two were rescued. Luckily, Layla and Jovan were safe and had received only minor injuries.

Layla and Jovan recovered after a few days in the hospital. Layla could not forgive herself for what she had done. She cried, hugging Jovan and pleading for his forgiveness. "I am so sorry, Love, I am so sorry." She bawled as she pressed him closer to his chest.

"It's okay, Mommy," mumbled Jovan with dewy eyes as he wiped away her tears. That evening Layla called a drug rehabilitation centre in New York and booked herself in for an eight-week treatment starting in three weeks' time. She also called her parents and informed them of her plan. They were very happy to hear about her decision and looked forward to having Layla and Jovan over. They could not wait to spend time with their grandson, show him around, take him to the movies and to the park, and buy him toys and Spiderman clothes. They wanted to show him off amongst relatives and friends, walking him around the hotel empire, his grandfather had built.

A week later, Jenna arrived in Poona to spend two months of her summer holidays with her mother and brother. Her mother informed her why her holiday needed to get cut down to one week this time, instead of two months. She also informed Jenna that she might take her to New York along with Jovan, to spend time with her maternal grandparents—after seeking Dadu and Dadi ma's permission. Jovan and Jenna were very excited and could not wait to visit their maternal grandparents.

After a week of fun and play, Jenna, Jovan, and Layla packed their bags. Layla left the house keys with Lakshmi, bid goodbye to her ashram friends, sought Bhagwan's blessings, and left for Chandigarh.

All of Layla's plans blew up in a smoke after she was caught with five kilograms of heroin from her house in Chandigarh.

Chapter 17
The End

This is the end, my only friend, the end.
It hurts to set you free,
But you'll never follow me.
The end of laughter and soft lies,
The end of nights we tried to die.
This is the end.
— *Jim Morrison*

2005

After Layla was caught that fateful night, the court had eventually proven her guilty of partnership in all of Riccardo's crimes. Upon hearing the shattering news of Layla's arrest, her parents flew down to India, but despite hiring a renowned lawyer to fight her case, they could not save her from a lifetime sentence behind bars. Layla had paid with 20 long years of her life for crime she had committed unwillingly, in a zombie-like state. After Layla was sentenced, no one came to see her in jail except her parents and her little children in Sohan Singh's company. Dadu and Dadi ma never visited her because it was against their morals to visit a jail. Riccardo had been deported to Italy a long time back. Layla had hated and cursed him, but she had eventually forgiven him. After going through the pain of repentance, she had finally resigned herself to her fate and had made peace with her *karma*, which had taught her many important lessons that her mature soul would carry into her next life. She had been strong enough to get over her addiction and had meditated every day since her incarceration. She listened to the *Bhagavad Gita* every morning and meditated with a clear mind. She lived on hope. She hoped of her release from jail one day, and of her union with her two loving children, who were now grown up and living as fine individuals, serving the world and those in need.

"Let's understand the root cause of all addiction. The root cause of all addiction lies is pain. All drugs are nothing more than pain killers. We live in a world that desires instant gratification and instant cures. People take drugs to instantly escape from the pain that they feel. The pain could be of abuse, rejection, failure, or simply the pain of living a humdrum, boring, and a monotonous life. There is a great old saying: 'Whatever you do, do not try to escape from your pain but be with it, live it and get over it.' How can the addicted live with their pain and recover? That is possible only if the world shows them love, compassion, and acceptance. Those addicted to drugs are usually shunned by society, are shown antipathy, and are looked down upon as irresponsible or a nuisance. We must understand that addiction is a disease. Let's not ostracise and shun those who are addicted to drugs. Let's love them, accept them, and help them recover."

The hall echoed with the sound of cheering and clapping as Dr. Jenna Sandhu, an author and medical practitioner specialising in psychology and the study and treatment of substance abuse and addictions, delivered her talk at one of the renowned halls of San Francisco. As she walked off the stage, people surrounded her for autographs. She meandered through the crowds with a smile on her face as she signed the copies of her latest book on addiction.

Jenna had grown up in her paternal grandparents' care. Her brother Jovan had moved to New York with their maternal grandparents.

Jenna and Jovan kept in close touch and spent two months of their summer holidays together every year, partly in India and mostly in New York. They wrote to Layla every week and sent her their pictures as they transitioned from childhood to adulthood. They shared their joys, sorrows, pains, and pleasures with her through their long letters. Layla wrote back to her children regularly, guiding and mentoring them through her letters. She taught them lessons that a lifetime of chaos, destruction, wrong association, and misfortune had taught her. She asked for their forgiveness for the suffering they had to go through due to mistakes made on her part. Jovan and Jenna loved their mother, and they stayed open to the wisdom she imparted upon them and absorbed it like sponges. They had suffered much, but their suffering had not been futile; it had been instrumental in their growth as wise, fine individuals of society who contributed to the betterment of the world.

After her schooling in Chandigarh, Jenna was sent to the United States to study medicine at one of the top universities. She graduated with flying colours and became a renowned doctor in the United States. She had met a charming young man during her university years, and the two had married and were now settled in San Francisco, practicing medicine and serving the world.

After delivering her talk, Jenna drove over the rolling hills of San Francisco. She was heading back home. Jenna now lived in the same Victorian house that her mother had lived in 38 years back, in the late 1960s during the Summer of Love and her wild university years. Jenna now lived here with her doting husband. As she drove down Lombard Street with its eight hairpin turns, her thoughts hovered around her mother, whose tumultuous life resembled this most crooked street in the world. Jenna thought of stopping by at the Red Victorian Café for a warm cup of coffee and running some errands before returning home.

Scott McKenzie's "San Francisco" played in the Red Victorian Café as Jenna entered, opening its creaky oak door. The song played, and it carried Jenna down the rabbit hole to memory lane, into the arms of her mother, and to the times when Jenna was not even born. She carried a vivid imagination of those times. The song carried her into her mother's youth, when she was not yet a mother. When Layla did become a mother, she often hummed these lines. The song played as Jenna grew up. The song played around their house in Poona, in the car, in the background everywhere—and today, in the Red Victorian Café.

Along with the mesmerizing spell of the song, the soothing aroma of coffee instantly eased Jenna's stressed-out nerves as she walked towards the cashier behind the counter, engulfed by warm, earthly hues. The café had been partly renovated from the time when it was a corner hangout for her mother and her flock of flowered friends. The old, worn-down wood beneath her beige high heels squeaked as Jenna leaned over and ordered. "One small café mocha, please." The cashier handed her the warm cup, and she cupped her hands around it and started walking swiftly towards the sitting area. Surrounded by small wooden round tables and chairs, a mammoth sofa, and a gigantic tea table, she quickly plopped herself on to a small plush corner sofa next to a large window that stayed partly open. Her dark brown hair flowed around her forehead and shoulders as the whispering wind gently caressed her face. Attired formally in a beige knee-length skirt and a beige blazer, she wrapped her colourful silk scarf around her neck to keep herself cosy in the cool breeze of San Francisco. Her olive complexion and piercing brown eyes reflected the looks of her father, Gary.

After settling down, she observed, as she had done innumerable times before, the paintings and framed pictures of John Lennon, the Who, Janis Joplin, and other artists who had fuelled the hippie movement, along with a large central portrait of a band of hippies gathered around one of the café tables smiling, blowing kisses, and making peace signals at the camera. Layla was one of them, looking wild, beautiful, and stoned. These historic artefacts adorning the red brick walls made this friendly old café feel like an ode to a bygone era, an era in which Layla had lived and loved.

Jenna hazily looked out of the window and at the street lined by the high-end shops, vintage clothing stores, exclusive boutiques, book stores, hip restaurants and bars, and thrift stores selling books and records—all paying homage to that history. Over 38 years later, the Summer of Love still lived on in this charming Victorian sector of San Francisco, where tourists roamed around and picked up relics in the forms of clothing, souvenirs, and memorabilia. This is where it had all began, where it all started in the summer of 1967. People adorned in beads, feathers, flowers, and bells, with garlands around their necks, played flutes and guitars. They were long-haired, were full of passion and rebellion, and roamed the streets of Haight Ashbury, just like her mother.

Jenna finished her coffee and walked out of the café. She strolled the street of Haight Ashbury. As she started walking towards the parking lot, she noticed the sky turn tar black and quickened her pace. Large pillows of clouds were forming, and light drizzle suddenly gave way to a thunderous downpour. People ran for cover, and umbrellas opened as the grey clouds spilled their beads of water. Jenna took off her blazer and lifted it over her head as she ran for shelter in to nearest thrift shop. She sat down on the high wooden bar stool politely offered by the shopkeeper. The shop was full of music records and posters of the pop stars of the old eras. A fancy poster displaying images of the Monterey Pop Festival caught her eye. Jenna still had pictures of her mom doing the Hippy Hippy Shake in the Monterey Pop Festival. She smiled. Just then, her cell phone rang. "Hello? Hi, Dadu! How are you?" Jenna answered her phone cheerfully.

A moment later, her smile gave way to a look of shock and horror. She cried, "What?"

After moving to New York with his grandparents at the age of 7, Jovan lived a safe life full of love and affection. Layla's parents tried to make up for the years of neglect that their daughter had gone through while they were busy making money and expanding their business across the country. After completing his schooling, Jovan joined a renowned university and received his master's degree in Business Administration and Hotel Management. He took over his grandfather's vast business. His grandparents now lived a retired life and spent their time travelling around the globe while he managed the Smith Group of York Hotels.

During his growing years, Jovan experienced anguish when he thought about the wretched life of deceit and lies that his father had lived. He felt angered at the fact that his mother was forced to spend a lifetime behind bars due to his father's selfish motives. Jovan had heard through the media that his father now lived as a free man in Italy, but his father had never once attempted to reach out, be it during his jail time or after his release. Jovan had no desire to meet him or to see him. Rather, he wanted to stay away from his sinister shadow.

To maintain his peace of mind, Jovan had grown up reading books on spirituality, especially Daoism and Buddhism. He had meditated regularly and for long hours during his adolescent years. As an adult, along with establishing himself as a successful businessman, he also became a philanthropist and a practicing Buddhist.

Jovan and Jenna, in mutual collaboration, opened up drug rehabilitation centres around the world in the name of their mother. They actively raised funds for the foundation and provided free care to those in need. While touring their rehab centres, Jenna lectured on the causes and cures of addiction, whereas Jovan spread words of wisdom and peace, stressing the importance of right living.

"Let's try to understanding the Fifth Precept of Buddhism, which deals with avoiding intoxicants. Intoxicant intake in excess blurs the mind. It takes away the mind's clarity and forces us to do things that we would never do in a sober state. Also, it creates an addictive cycle of craving, as is illustrated by the realm of Hungry Ghosts in the Buddhist Wheel of Life," explained Jovan to a group of people in recovery at one of his rehabilitation centres in New York.

He stood tall and lean like his mother, and he looked noble while attired in a white shirt and beige khakis. His short blond hair was neatly trimmed, his deep blue eyes reflected love and compassion for humanity, and his well-built torso hid a kind and soft heart. His words spilt wisdom while he explained the Buddhist Wheel of Life, as depicted on the slide behind him. A beaded mala was wrapped around his wrist as he pointed towards the slide and explained. "Each realm in this Wheel of Life is occupied by characters representing certain aspects of human existence. The inhabitants of the Hungry Ghost realm are depicted as creatures with thin and long necks, tiny mouths, bony and wasted limbs, and bloated and hollow bellies. These are the addicts, and this is the realm of addiction where people are constantly seeking something outside of themselves to repress an insatiable yearning for gratification and fulfilment. The emptiness and hunger is not satisfying because the substances that they consume, hoping for fulfilment, are delusional and increase the hunger even more."

Jovan's speech was disrupted by a knock on the classroom door. "Sorry to disturb you, Sir, but there's an urgent phone call for you," said the receptionist.

"Thank you. I'll be right there," said Jovan. "Excuse me, friends," he apologized to the class full of anxious, engaged listeners battling the demon of addiction. He walked out of the classroom to attend to the phone call. It was Jenna on the other end of the line.

"Jovan, Mommy is no more ... She passed away last night. She had a heart attack." Jenna sobbed and sniffed. Jovan stood still as he listened. His body felt numb and lifeless as Jenna continued "I am leaving for India tonight. The Delhi jail authorities are going to move her body to the Chandigarh Hospital morgue from Delhi."

Jovan cleared the lump in his throat and managed to say, "I'll take the next flight to Delhi. You take care of yourself, Jenna." Jovan gave a display of feigned strength. His eyes brimmed with tears, and his heart ached as he hung up.

Jovan and Jenna reached Delhi around the same time. Jenna, who had arrived a few hours before Jovan, was waiting for him at the airport lounge. Jovan, dressed in denims and a white T-shirt, walked swiftly towards the lounge as his blue eyes searched for his sister. His eyes rested on a figure of a young woman waving at him from a distance. It was Jenna, with dark brown hair and olive skin. Jovan's vision blurred due to the tears in his eyes as she rushed towards him with open arms. Jenna hugged him and cried as he rubbed her back and kissed her. "It's okay, Jenna. Birth and death have their timings that no one can control," he said as he caressed her back. They walked out of the airport gates. It was 11:00 p.m., and the familiar heat of June welcomed the two with its warmth and humidity. The full moon seemed blurred, engulfed in the smog-filled air. Horns blared, and the traffic crawled on the road as their eyes swiftly browsed over some 10 men holding placards with people's names.

A distant turbaned figure waved and glided hurriedly towards the two. It was Sohan Singh . He walked towards the two with dewy eyes. "Sat Sri Akal, baby and *kaka ji*," he greeted, with folded palms, moist eyes, and a choked-up throat.

"Sat Sri Akal, Sohan Uncle," replied Jovan and Jenna as they tenderly hugged him. Sohan Singh placed his hand over their heads and blessed the two with a deep sigh and a heavy heart. He had grown older and weaker and now sported a full grey beard. Jovan pushed the baggage trolley to the nearby parking lot and followed Sohan Singh, who walked briskly in front of the two, leading the way. They approached the old black Mercedes, Jovan slid in the suitcases, the two stepped inside the car, and off they were on their way to Chandigarh.

Jenna lay her fatigued head on Jovan's shoulder and held his hand as they drove to Chandigarh. They passed by the roadside *Dhabas* and crossed the colourful trucks, flooding their minds with memories of the bygone days. They drove on to the wide-open streets of Chandigarh under a canopy of lush green trees. Familiar landmarks greeted them: the *Tribune* building, the Sikh temple, the lake. Soon Sohan Singh parked in front of the majestic arched gate of the Sandhu mansion. The bronze name plate that read "The Sandhus," hanging on one side of the black metallic gate, seemed dull and lustreless. Birds twittered around bushes, and black crows cawed while perched on the branches of green mango trees. The rising sun peeked through the tall Ashoka trees, lighting the sky in its pink and orange hues. Mrs. Sharma, the neighbour, now older and skinnier, was engaged in *Surya Namaskar* as the two stepped out of the car. She blessed the two from her rooftop with one eye on them as she offered water to the sun and bowed reverently.

Sohan Singh rang the doorbell. Kashi Ram and Bali Ram opened the main gate. They bowed and blessed Jenna and Jovan with moist eyes and quivering lips while leading them towards the main door. Dadi ma opened the front door with shaky hands and tearful green eyes. Dadu, who stood beside her, still looked tall and strong. Dadi ma now seemed frail and weak and supported herself with a walking stick as she staggered out the door. Jenna rushed towards the two, hugged them, and cried in their arms as they blessed, caressed, and kissed her. Jovan bent over and touched their feet as the two blessed and hugged him.

A few close family members had already gathered in the house, including Jenna's Aunt Jasmine and Jasmine's mother. Layla's parents arrived from New York a little later that morning. They hugged Jenna and Jovan with heavy hearts and brimming eyes. Jenna, Jovan, and Layla's parents freshened up and then left for the hospital morgue to collect Layla's body. Memories of Layla fogged their minds as they approached the hospital.

Long, sad, and stressed faces loomed around the corridors of the hospital, which smelled of disinfectant mixed with rubbing alcohol. A staff member walked them down to the morgue that echoed the transitory nature of human life and emitted a fetid smell that overwhelmed their senses. Surrounded by unclaimed dead bodies lying in cold chambers, the four cautiously walked behind the attendant, who scanned the bodies lying in drawers. He identified Layla's body by a toe tag that was attached to the big toe of her right foot. On the tag was inscribed her name, Layla Smith Sandhu, and her case number.

As the attendant pulled out the drawer, Jovan, Jenna, and their grandparents watched over Layla with moist eyes, trembling hands, and quivering lips. Her face seemed calm and serene. Wisdom reflected in the creases of her face. She lay there in peace and silence, seeming like an epitome of patience and forbearance. Her soul had travelled far across the universe, along with its wisdom and karma, while her body lay here, reduced to a mere number and a name, a life that had learnt many tough lessons and had suffered more than it deserved. Layla, their mother, was now gone.

Jovan hugged Jenna as he caressed her and whispered, "Do not worry, Jenna. Our mother has gone to a better place. She is finally free and liberated, and she is no longer paying for the sins of others. Stay strong Jenna. Her life will not go unnoticed or be futile. Many lives and families will be served and saved in her memory."

Jenna buried her face in Jovan's chest as she sobbed and whispered, "Yes!"

Layla had expressed her desire to be cremated instead of being buried. She wished to be cremated in the same ground as Gary. As per Layla's wishes, her body was taken to the house, where she was washed, bathed, and dressed in fresh new clothes. Incense was burned next to her body as the prayers were recited. Dadu, Dadi ma, Layla's parents, and a few other close members of the family escorted the body to the cremation ground. The last prayers were sung as the body was placed on the pyre. Jovan lit the pyre, and all-consuming, tall, orange and yellow flames flared up towards the sky, burning everything in a grey smoke. Jenna and Jovan held on to one another as they watched the flames. The flames seemed to sparkle and reach the sky. Little embers took the shape of twinkling stars ascending to the heavens above. For now, their mother was in the stars above, sprinkling her blessing down upon them like diamonds. As the flames subdued, the two turned their backs against the pyre, wrapped their arms around one another, and walked away with dreams, aspirations, and hopes burning in their aching hearts. Much was yet to be done and accomplished. Many lives and families were yet to be saved and served in memory of their mother, Layla.

CPSIA information can be obtained
at www.ICGtesting.com
Printed in the USA
LVHW02s1449240718
584774LV00001B/146/P